They Found Us

Joy Mullett

J M Publications Limited

To my family and friends who have always believed in me.
To you, the reader, thank you for giving my work a chance.
To the universe, for making my dreams come true.

Contents

Authors Note

Please be aware, this book is intended for mature audiences ages 18 and over.

The story includes open door romance, along with some darker themes, including violence and murder.

However, there are many happy and romantic scenes.

If you are okay with this, please continue and enjoy.

Joy x

Books in this series:

This book 'They Found Us' is book 5 in The Found Series. This book cannot be read as a standalone. Please ensure you have read the previous books in this series first.

I've Found Her-Bella and Damien
I've Found Her part two- Chloe and Josh
He Found Me- Katie and Leo
She Found Me- Marco and Mia
They Found Us-Katie and Leo

With more to come later in the year.

All books are available on Amazon.

Follow Joy on social media for her latest releases and updates.

Chapter One

Leo

"Good morning, handsome." Katie lies facing me, her hand between her face and the pillow. God, she's beautiful.

"I've been thinking," she starts as soon as she sees me awake, "there are still a few things we need to get for the baby. Nappies, some formula just in case I need help feeding, more clothes, bibs —definitely bibs." Katie continues to chatter on, more to herself than me. Her voice is soft but raspy, as she's just woken up. I could listen to her talk for hours.

"We will go today and get whatever you need." I know we don't really need anything, as there's a wardrobe full of clothes and drawers packed with nappies. But if that's what my wife wants to do today, then who am I to argue. She is carrying my second child. Her beauty and voice have my morning wood pulsing. I disappear under the covers and nestle between her legs. I'm just about to work my magic when a whack to the back has me faceplanting the mattress.

"Papa, are you hiding from me?" Mark continues to jump on my back.

"That's enough now. Let's leave Papa to rest for a few minutes while we go and get the breakfast ready."

Katie lifts the covers and climbs out of bed.

"Sorry," she whispers. "Come down when you're ready." She looks at my crotch area covered by the duvet.

Definitely best to stay here. I don't fancy having that conversation with my three-year-old son. Once I have thought of everything under the sun other than my wife, I'm ready to go downstairs.

"Your coffee is ready, Leo," Katie shouts up.

"Thanks. On my way now."

I throw on some sweatpants and meet my family in the kitchen. Katie stands at the sink, her back to me, I take a moment to enjoy the sight of her perfectly round ass bursting to get out of her tiny shorts. She is quietly narrating what she is doing and what her next plans are for the day.

"I'll just finish these pots, then I'll collect the eggs for breakfast, and then we can all go to the baby shop..."

It's like she has her own personal podcast

and I'm her number one listener. My hands are on her ass before I even know what I am doing, my face in the side of her neck, breathing in her scent.

"Hey." She spins around, kisses me, then pushes me away with her wet hands.

I just can't help myself. When I'm around her, all I want to do is touch her.

"Mark and I are going to collect the eggs. You put the pan on with boiling water and slice some bread for toast. Mark has requested egg in a cup for us all this morning."

"Yes, egg in a cup, egg in a cup!" He jumps about excitedly.

They both go out into the garden and collect today's eggs from the chicken coop. I do as I am asked, slicing the bread and get the pan ready. Egg in a cup is something I had never had before meeting Katie. It's a boiled egg, or two, mashed up in a cup with butter and it bit of salt and pepper. We have it on toast. Don't knock it till you've tried it. It's one of my favourite breakfasts now.

I watch from the back door as my wife feeds the chickens and Mark the billy goats. They both talk to them like they are people but in funny, squeaky voices. Mark just copies everything Katie says. They return with the eggs, wash their hands, and we all work together to set the table and prepare the food.

Katie

When we arrive at the baby shop, Mark gets instantly distracted by some sort of toy and runs in that direction. Leo insisted he didn't need his reins on for the shopping trip even though Mark has started to be a little unpredictable. "I'll be there" was his reasoning as if he has some magical powers to control children.

"You keep an eye on him while I get what we need," I say sarcastically, giving him a "I told you so" look.

I grab a trolley and make my way around the shop. My eyes dart over the pastel-coloured baby clothes, tiny hats, and booties. The air smells of baby powder and excitement while nursery rhymes play quietly in the background. I can't help but smile as I imagine my newborn. I load up the trolley with neutral baby outfits, nappies, and toiletries. I think I am just about done when Leo appears in front of me.

"We *have* to get these," he says excitedly holding two matching outfits.

"Absolutely not. Why would a newborn and a three-year-old need a black three-piece suit, shirt, and tie?"

"You never know. We might get invited to an occasion."

"By who?" I ask, but then notice that the excitement that was there a moment ago has started to fade. "Put them in the trolley. They are very cute."

Then I ask, "Leo. Where is Mark?" My eyes dart frantically around us. "Mark!" my voice comes out strangled as I call his name. I force myself to breathe and think. "You go and alert the staff. Get them to make an announcement." Leo marches off to the customer service desk while I rush up and down each aisle.

"Have you seen a dark-haired three-year-old boy?" I ask the unfamiliar faces of each shopper I pass.

"No, sorry," they all reply.

Continuing to shout his name over the noise of the shop that now seems ten times louder, my heart slams against my ribs.

"He's here somewhere," I tell myself. "He will be near the toys."

"Mark Smith. Your parents are looking for you. Please shout, 'I'm here' as loud as you can. Mark Smith, please shout, 'I'm here' as loud as you can."

I stop, keeping as still as I can to listen for my son. But all I can hear are those stupid nursery rhymes and people talking.

When I get to the toys, I know he's here. Call it a mothers' intuition, but I feel calmer. "Mark, where are you? We need to get going now, and you haven't chosen what toy you would like yet."

Immediately the pile of soft toys beside me falls, and out jumps Mark.

"Boo!" He laughs. "Did I scare you, Mummy? Did I scare you?"

My knees buckle in relief. I hold on to the shelf at the side of me for a second to stop me from falling. "Oh yes, you definitely scared me, baby." I scoop him up and swallow back tears.

Leo appears and looks instantly relieved when his eyes land on Mark. "You two get in the car. I'll pay for the shopping."

When we get home, I still can't shift the uneasy feeling in my stomach. It's like a sense of dread, but I don't know what for. We found Mark, and he is perfectly fine. I put all the shopping away in the nursery. Everything has its place and is organised and tidy. Not that it will stay like this for long once the baby is here. Once that was done, Leo insisted I sit with my feet up. At first I refused, but I must have been tired, as Leo and Mark have just woken me up by bursting in through the back door, carrying a ball.

"Mummy, have you had a good nap?" Mark

climbs on me, being careful not to stand on my bump.

"I did, thank you. And where have you two been?"

"To the beach to play football."

"I'll make dinner tonight. Spaghetti bolognese?" Leo wiggles his eyebrows at me, making me laugh.

He knows I can't resist him when he cooks Italian food. There's just something about an Italian man, especially a very attractive Italian man serving you delicious Italian food. My mouth waters already. Spag bol, as I used to call it and am banned from calling it now, used to be such a boring dish to me. But I had never tasted a real bolognese made by an Italian. The recipe Leo follows is one he got from Sergio and Alga, our chef and housekeeper from Italy. They said the recipe had been in their family for years. I often think about Alga and Sergio. They were more like family to us. I miss them.

Mark sits and colours at the table beside me while I watch Leo begin to work his magic in the kitchen. He puts on his apron and rolls up his sleeves, showing off his olive-toned forearms. As he chops and dices the ingredients, the kitchen is soon filled with the scent of sizzling onions, garlic, and herbs. He puts the beef into the pan next, then the tomatoes. As he stirs, he coaxes out more delicious flavours. Then he opens a bottle of red wine, pours himself a glass, and the rest goes into the pan. Turning down the heat, he says "Low and slow. That's what Sergio always said."

Once it's ready, we sit around the table. Leo sprinkles our bowls with freshly grated parmesan, and steam curls up from our forks when we dig in. The first mouthful is always the best, warm, rich, and familiar. The kitchen is silent while each of us enjoys our food. But the silence is soon disturbed by a ringing noise that will change our lives forever.

Chapter Two

Katie

Leo and I both stop mid-mouthful and look at each other. It takes a moment for me to register where the noise is coming from. Leo stands quickly, his chair making a high-pitched screech on the floor with the force.

He opens the cupboard in the corner of the kitchen, reaches in, and pulls out a red telephone receiver. "Yes?"

I watch Leo's expression, trying to read him. I can't hear anything from the other end of the phone call. Leo notices me look at him intently and turns his back on me. I release my fork from my hand, no longer hungry. That phone has never rung since we've been here. To be honest, I had forgotten it was there. When we first moved in, Leo installed it as an absolute emergency phone. I thought that it was for us to use if we ever needed help here. I never for one moment thought that someone would ring us.

"What's happened?" I ask when he puts down the receiver. Leo hadn't said much in reply, just the odd "When?" and "Where?"

"It's nothing for you to be concerned about."

But that's the understatement of the century.

"Then why have we just had a phone call?" I ask as I make my way towards him to look him in the eyes.

"Van needed some advice, that's all," he replies without looking at me.

"Leo, we are supposed to be dead. It is out of our control." Leo had hardly said a word, so where was this advice Van so desperately needed?

A frown I haven't seen for years crosses his brow. I knew something strange was going to happen today. I sensed it. I've felt uneasy all day. We should never have had to install that phone in the first place.

Deciding that now is not the time to push for more answers, I say, "Let's sit down and finish our dinner." I return to the table and sit next to Mark, who has almost finished his spaghetti bolognese. His cheeks and hands are stained orange, evidence of him having thoroughly enjoyed it.

"No, I'm not hungry. I need to think." Leo opens the top cupboard in the kitchen and pulls out a tin. He removes the lid and takes out a cigar and lighter.

I watch as he lights it, the smoke instantly encircling his head. The sight brings back memories of a very different time in our lives. It's years since I've seen him smoke. He quit when we moved onto Nuova Vita Island.

After a moment of remembering how we came to be together, I realise the seriousness of what he is doing. "Leo, get outside with that. Don't let Mark breathe it in!" *Or me,* I think, as I rub my heavily pregnant stomach.

Leo suddenly pulls himself from his distraction and realises his mistake. "Sorry."

I open the door and usher Leo out, wafting the smoke along with him.

After I've finished my dinner and cleared the table, Leo returns with the same worried frown. He seems distant.

"Come on, let's take Mark out for a walk," I say, trying to bring Leo out of his dark thoughts.

Every evening after dinner, we take Mark out for a walk in his pram. The boy is a live wire, and this routine really helps settle him down ready for bed.

But I'm surprised as Leo declines, it's something we have always done together.

"You go, I'll see you when you get back." He

kisses me on the forehead, does the same with Mark, and then disappears through the house. I hear him close his office door and lock it behind him.

Leaving Leo to gather his thoughts, I get Mark's shoes on and manoeuvre his pushchair out of the backdoor. We usually walk along the beachfront, letting Mark toddle the first half to tire him out, then put him in this pushchair for the way back. We've been for a walk every evening since Mark was born. Mark doesn't seem phased, however, that his Papa isn't coming, so we set off down the path that leads from our home to the beach.

The air is definitely cooler today. The sky is overcast, but it's far from cold. We reach the beachfront in minutes. I push the chair along the path while Mark stomps and skips in the sand beside me. After a few metres, the pushchair gets stuck in a raised plank on the path. I pull and push, trying to release it, but it just gets wedged in tighter. Struggling to bend down with my huge baby bump, I grab hold of the wheel and give it a wiggle. But still no luck. Standing tall again so my lungs have room to expand, I realise Mark is no longer at my side.

Searching frantically around me, I spot him running straight towards the ocean. "Mark! Stop!" I shout, but he doesn't listen. I'm running full throttle in panic, holding my bump as I go. When

I'm not pregnant, I'm fit. I run a lot, and I'm fast, much to Leo's annoyance, as I can beat him in a race by miles. But right now, my lungs are burning as I pant to breathe, and the pain in my stomach has me worrying about my unborn child.

The gap between me and Mark is closing but not fast enough. He is almost at the water. Mark can swim, and we often take him swimming in the sea, but today the sea is rougher than usual, and the waves crashing on the beach would soon pull him in. I then notice a woman running along the shore, close to Mark. I frantically shout and wave my arms to get her attention. Thankfully she notices, and I point over to Mark while still running desperately. The woman picks up her running pace and manages to lift him up just as he reaches the water. Thank goodness.

Seconds later I catch up to them. The lady passes me Mark, who kicks and whines in protest of being stopped from going for a paddle.

"Oh, thank you so much," I say to the dark-haired woman who looks a similar age to me. "Thank goodness you got to him in time. I had visions of him being swept out to sea. Don't ever run away from Mummy again, Mark. That could have been very dangerous. Look how rough the sea is. Now say sorry and thank you to the lady."

Mark folds his arms and pushes out his bottom lip. "Sorry. Thank you."

"You are very welcome," she replies in a strong accent I know very well. She is a very beautiful lady. Her dark eyes and olive skin remind me of Mia. Wow, I haven't thought of her in a long time.

"Oh, is that an Italian accent I hear?"

Her smile fades slightly before she says, "Mi dispiace di non parlare molto inglese." *I'm sorry I do not speak much English.*

Before I can reply, she sets off running. Struggling with a now-crying three-year-old, I let her leave and put Mark down on the sand, keeping a secure grip on his wrist as I speak to him firmly about the importance of not running off and listening to Mummy. Not that he takes much notice.

When we get back to his pushchair, I strap him in tightly. Thankfully with another few pulls, the wheel becomes unstuck. Having had enough exercise for one night, I make my way back to the house. When we arrive home, I go looking for Leo. His office door is now open, but it's empty. As I call out for him, I hear the sound of his footsteps coming down the stairs. When he approaches me in the hall, my breath is taken away. Leo's appearance sends butterflies to my stomach. His natural beard has been trimmed and shaped, and his hair is no longer in its loose natural waves—it's slick back with not a piece out of place. He is the image of when we first met. But the flood of sexual excitement is soon replaced with dread, as I realise what this means.

He is going back.

Chapter Three

Katie

"No. Absolutely not, Leo. You can't be serious?"

"I have no choice. Marco needs me." Leo doesn't look at me when he speaks.

"You do have a choice. *We* need you, Leo. We left that world behind, and for good reason."

Leo walks around me and goes into the kitchen. I follow him, wincing as I go as the pains in my stomach return.

"Tell me what is going on. Tell me what is so important that you would take your family back to Italy, a place we had to fake our own deaths to escape from."

Leo turns to face me. His expression is stern. "I'm going alone. You will stay here."

"No, you are not leaving us. If you are going, so are we." I look at Mark, who has fallen asleep in his chair. "I'll pack us some things. How long do you think we will gone?" I go to the cupboard and get out Mark's lunch bag and start filling it with snacks and drinks for the journey.

"Stop!" Leo demands, making me jump.

I look at Mark, but he is still sound asleep.

"I am going alone. It is not safe for you and Mark. You will do as I say, *Kat-er-een!*"

The way he says my name send shivers down my spine. Leo has not called me by my full name like this since we arrived on the island. Well, apart from when he throws me on the bed dominantly during our lovemaking sessions. But this is different. This is the old Leo. The Leo I chose to forget.

"Leo, you are scaring me." I bow my head in sadness. This is my worst nightmare come true.

Leo walks towards me and takes my hands in his. "I'm sorry." He tilts my chin up to look into my eyes. "Please, Katie. You need to trust me. I'm going to go back and help Marco. I'll be gone two, three days maximum. Nobody will even know I'm there. I will do what needs to be done, and then I will come home, and we will continue our happily ever after." He cups my cheeks and kisses me softly. "Promesso." *I promise*. He wipes my tears that have fallen with his thumbs.

I feel sick. I know this is not going to be as simple as he thinks. But I know there's no point arguing. When *this* Leo—the leader of the Guerra, Leo—puts his foot down, there's nothing I can do. And it is safer for me and Mark to stay here. I just wish he didn't have to go.

"When do you go?" I say, accepting defeat.

"There's a car coming in ten minutes." He pulls me into his arms as a sob leaves my chest. "I'll be back before you know it."

The next ten minutes pass extremely quickly. The thought of being without him breaks my heart.

"It's time to go," Leo says as he kisses our son. "Ti amo." *I love you.*

The sight of Leo saying goodbye to our sleeping son has tears once again rolling down my cheeks. Bloody pregnancy hormones. I'm not usually such an emotional wreck.

"I will ring you on the red phone every day at 9:00 a.m.," he instructs as he once again wipes the tears from my face.

"How will I contact you?"

"You won't. It's the safest way. I don't want anything to lead back here to you." After rubbing my tummy and giving me a kiss I never want to end, he leaves the safety of our home without looking back.

This can't be happening. It's all happened too fast. It feels like a bad decision. I should have fought harder to make him stay.

As I close the door, I hear Mark starting to stir, so I wipe my eyes, take a deep breath, and switch into mummy mode. I carefully lift Mark from his pushchair, singing lullabies to soothe him. I carry him upstairs into his bedroom and gently change him into his pyjamas. Once he is settled, I go into mine and Leo's room and climb into bed. Wrapping our covers around me, I let myself cry while inhaling the smell left by my husband. My mind runs wild. What if something happens to him? What if he never comes home? What if something happens to Mark, and I need him? How will I get hold of him? The what-if's continue as I wail into my pillow until I eventually fall asleep.

A few hours have passed by when I am woken by a sound. My eyes spring open, and I'm on high alert as I listen for the noise again. The room is now in complete darkness. It must be well into the early hours of the next morning. A moment or two passes before I hear it again. It's a rattle or tapping sound. I start to panic. What if Leo has been caught already, and someone is here to get me and Mark?

Mark.

The thought of my son puts me in fight mode. I'm out of bed and in Mark's bedroom before I can think. His room has a nightlight, so I can easily see he is safely sleeping in his bed. I hear the noise again. It's coming from downstairs. Quietly I close his bedroom door and tiptoe down. There it is again. It's coming from the kitchen. I stop on the bottom stair and quickly plan my next move. Generally I'm fit and strong. Leo taught me self-defence years ago when we first moved here, and I can take Leo down without a problem. But I'm currently eight months pregnant.

I know what I have to do. I sneak into Leo's office and open his safe. Thank goodness. I thought he might have taken it with him. My adrenaline kicks in as I hold the cold steel in my hand. I check the chamber and find it loaded. Taking the safety off, I make my way out of the office, keeping my back to the wall with both hands on the gun out in front of me like Leo taught me.

As I approach the kitchen, I hear the noise again. I then see shadows across the back door. Taking a deep breath, I enter the kitchen and search each corner as I make my way closer to the door. The moonlight shines in through our open blinds. The kitchen is empty. The noise again has me spinning in the direction of the door. Through the window, I see the shadow of tree branches. I then hear the sound of the wind whistling through our vineyard. Peering out of the window, I see one of the olives trees has fallen by the door. Its pot is broken, and the branches tap on the door as the wind picks up again.

My heart starts to calm as I check the door is indeed locked. Just to be sure, I switch on the lights in each room and check there is no one else here. All clear. After I have carefully returned the gun to the safe, I sit down at the kitchen table with a glass of water. I could murder a gin and tonic right now.

The sound of Mark stirring upstairs brings me out of my thoughts. I turn everything off and double-check the doors are locked before I go to Mark, who wants a sleepy cuddle from his mummy. Feeling like I also need some comfort, I take him into our room and settle us both in bed. Mark is soon fast asleep again in my arms. I, on the other hand, am wide awake. Since arriving here three years ago, I have never felt anything other than safe. But now I feel incredibly vulnerable and scared. Even back in Italy, where I always knew I was in some sort of danger just through being with Leo, I never felt this fearful. Leo can't come home soon enough.

When Mark wakes up at 6:30 a.m., I'm still awake. We get up and start our usual routine. Breakfast for both of us, and then we get dressed and go out to feed the animals. There's a little more to do this morning after last night's winds. Thankfully the animals are okay. The weather today, however, is back to the usual calm, blue skies and sunshine. At 8:55, I go back inside and wait for the phone to ring. Five minutes is a long time when you are waiting for something. At 9:00

21

a.m. on the dot, the phone rings.

"Leo?" I ask, longing to hear his voice.

"Katie. How are you? How is Mark?"

"We are both fine. How are you? What's going on there? Are you safe?"

"I'm safe. I only have a minute. Please do not worry, la mia ragazza." *My girl.* You are safe there. I will be home soon. Take care. I will ring you tomorrow morning at 9:00. Make sure you answer."

"I will be waiting for your call."

"Ti amo." *I love you.*

"Ti amo," I reply as he ends the call.

Holding back the tears, I take Mark outside again.

We spend a few hours clearing the broken pots and fallen branches as well as cleaning outing the chickens and goats. Mark loves our two billy goats, Upsy and Daisy, named after his favourite TV show at the time. He loves the outdoors. I can't wait for him to have a little brother or sister to play with.

When we go inside for lunch, Mark makes his usual mess with half of his food on the floor. Once he has finished, I put him down for his nap. While he is sleeping, I clear up and get the goat's cheese and eggs packed up and ready to take to the market. We take our produce and exchange it for other homemade goodies once a week. I enjoy the social side of it. Although we have been here for a few years, we haven't made any friends as such. We know many people on the island, but only to talk to. I don't know anything about anyone even though I see them every week.

Then again, I don't suppose they know anything about us. Leo is very untrusting of everyone. I know he misses Marco. He was like brother to him after his only brother Alex died. Marco and Leo did everything together. Leo never speaks of him—or anything from our past lives, actually. But I know he thinks about him a lot. That's why I shouldn't be surprised he went to Marco's aid the minute he got the call.

When Mark wakes, I strap him into his pushchair. I don't want a repeat of last night. Mark is so much better behaved for Leo, especially now that I'm pregnant. He knows I'm not as fast and agile as I usually am. Little monkey.

The market is busy as usual. We go to the goods exchange stalls first, where I place our produce down and then let Mark choose some baked goods in return. We usually exchange for something sweet that Mark can enjoy, which keeps him occupied while we browse the items that are for sale. It feels very strange being here without Leo. Once Mark has chosen and he is happily eating one of his chocolate brownies, I pick some of our favourite fresh breads. Then we mix into the hustle and bustle to see if there is anything that takes my fancy. The baby stall catches my attention first. It's full of beautiful tiny handmade clothes and soft toys. Mark spots a blue crochet teddy bear he likes, so I have that, a blanket, and a knitted cardigan for the new baby bagged up and pay for them. At the next stall, I spot someone I recognise. It's the running lady from the beach that caught Mark.

"Hello, again," I say as I approach her. "I didn't get chance to thank you properly last night."

"Mi dispiace di non parlare inglese." *I'm sorry, I don't speak English.* She smiles and then turns to walk away.

"Va bene, parlo italiano." *That's okay, I speak Italian.*

The lady stops in her tracks and slowly turns back to look at me. Her expression is surprised and quizzical. "Non sembri italiana." *You don't look Italian.*

Her response makes me laugh. "Non sono." *I'm not.* I reply.

The lady gives me another smile, but it doesn't quite meet her eyes.

"Devo andare. Piacere di rivederti." *I need to go. Nice to see you again.* And then she goes, leaving me with many questions.

We stop for a coffee halfway around the market. Well, I have a coffee. Mark has a milkshake along with a fruit snack I packed. I'm sat at our table with my back to the entrance of the café. In the reflection of the fridge door, I can see anyone who enters. It's a cautious action Leo has drummed into me that has become natural now. Ensure that whenever we are in a resting position, we can see anyone approaching from behind. Always have eyes on the entrances and exits. Know how many people are in the immediate vicinity— six: two couples and two people sitting alone. Four females, two males. Stay alert without making it obvious that you are paying attention.

While chatting to Mark about his new soft toy, I notice a lady enter the café. She is greeted by one of the waiters, who shows her to a table. The first table in the middle of the café, she refuses. The next, one in a corner, she accepts. It's the Italian lady again. She speaks to the waiter for a few moments about the weather. He then asks what she would like to order, and they discuss the menu. In English. Fluent English. I thought it surprising that she didn't speak English well enough to speak to me. Although most of the people who live here aren't originally from the UK, it's the main language that everyone uses to communicate. I thought maybe she had just arrived. But no. It seems she just didn't want to talk to me.

Once Mark and I have finished our

refreshments, we make our way out of the café, purposely walking past the Italian lady. She looks in our direction as I approach.

Chapter Four

Katie

"You learn fast," I say sarcastically.

"Mi scusi?" *Excuse me*?

"English. I heard you speaking to the waiter. I was only trying to thank you earlier. There was no need to be rude."

She opens her mouth slightly to say something, but I leave before she can.

On our walk home, I'm annoyed with the ignorance of the lady. I only wanted a friendly bit of conversation. I miss my friends Bella and Emmaline. I miss my mum. Although she never had a bright piece of advice to give, I miss our conversations on the soaps or whatever trash we were watching on Netflix that week. We have a lovely life here, but I miss adult interaction and friendship.

When we arrive home, I try and shift my mindset and be grateful for all that we have and the life that our children will have. But it's hard not having Leo here.

After dinner I take Mark for our usual evening walk. Tonight, I have put his harness and reins on, much to his annoyance, but I'm not having a repeat of last night. I also push the pram on the sand so it wouldn't get stuck again. Thank goodness for sand wheels. We walk along the shore, and I let Mark have a paddle in the sea while holding tightly onto his reins.

I love the sea air, the fresh salty oxygen that fills your lungs more than city air does, and the sound of the waves crashing on shore. I love spending time on the beach, having picnics and making sandcastles for Mark to knock over. In Italy, I spent a lot of my time on the beach, either with Leo or Emmaline. The pregnancy, and then Leo leaving, has really brought back memories of our previous life. I think today is the first time in over three years that I have felt homesick.

When we're ready to go back home, I put Mark in his pushchair and cover him with a blanket. The evening air is getting much cooler now. As I'm pushing him along and singing softly, I hear fast footsteps approaching us from behind. I turn quickly keeping my stance strong, ready to protect.

Leo

My heart burns at the sight of my wife saying goodbye. Her eyes are filled with emotion and vulnerability. I feel physically sick leaving my whole world alone. I never thought I would have to leave. I'm not sure if I am making the right decision. But I know I couldn't live with myself if I did not.

When Van called, I knew I was his last hope. I had the emergency radio phone fitted for absolute catastrophic situations only. I thought it would never ring. I prayed it would never ring. In hindsight, I shouldn't have had it in the first place. But knowing it was there and not ringing, helped me enjoy my new life without feeling guilty for leaving. Now I feel gut-wrenching guilt for going back to Italy. My plan is to sort out the mess as soon as possible while remaining undetected and return in a couple days. I'm taking a massive risk going back there. Risking my life and my family's. I stop myself from thinking about what will happen to them if I am caught.

When the car starts, I don't look back at my beautiful wife cradling her stomach where our unborn child is growing. It's too painful. Instead, I put myself into work mode. A personality I have suppressed for years. As I let Van's words fill my mind, anger builds and adrenaline bursts through my veins. The Martelé have been recruiting since my departure, accepting any vile Neanderthal that came forward. They're out of control. It's a disgrace to the underworld, even for them.

Marco has lost his head and therefore the respect of Guerra men. I would have put my life on the fact that Marco could never fall for the opposite sex. But I shouldn't have underestimated the power women have. I'm a prime example of this. And if that woman is ripped from your heart, all sanity is ripped from you along with her.

I'm taken to the airbase and smuggled into a cargo plane. Then a ship takes me to Italy. It's a long, uncomfortable journey for which wearing a custom-made €10,000 suit isn't ideal. But it's my armour. It oozes power. Although the few people who see me during my transfer have no idea who I am, the suit speaks volumes, instructing them not to speak a word if they want to live.

When the van I've been travelling in opens its doors, I instantly know I'm back in Italy. The smell of the air tickles my nose, welcoming me back to the country that runs through my veins. Now the challenge begins. I'm dropped off a mile away from the Guerra house, just on the edge of the grounds. My task now is to make it to the house without being detected. Not even by Guerra men. No one must know I am alive.

Katie

My posture soon relaxes when I see who is approaching us. The Italian lady. I wait for her to catch us up.

"Hello. Thank you for waiting," she says a little breathlessly. "I'm so glad I have seen you again. I wanted to explain and apologise." Every word is spoken in perfect English with an Italian accent.

"Okay," I respond, letting her continue.

"My name is Giovanna, but everyone calls me Vanna." Vanna holds her hand out to introduce herself.

I accept. "I'm Katie."

"It's nice to meet you, Katie." She smiles genuinely. "Please accept my apologises for our previous encounters. I prefer to keep myself to myself, but I shouldn't have been rude."

"You and everyone else around here. We've lived here three years now, and I still don't know anyone to speak to, apart from passing conversation." I sigh, homesickness once again filling me.

Vanna smiles sympathetically. "You get used to it eventually."

"Have you lived here for a long time?"

"Yes, since I was about eighteen." She sighs.

Looking at Vanna, I'd say she was about my

age, in her early to mid-thirties.

"Do you have family here?" I ask, hoping I'm not overstepping.

"It's just me and my husband." Vanna replies, still smiling, but I can see sadness behind her eyes.

"Would you like to have a coffee some time? I could do with some adult conversation." I laugh, gesturing to little Mark asleep in his pushchair.

Vanna takes a moment to reply, and I think she is going to refuse, but then she says, "Yes, I would like that."

Vanna sounds genuinely pleased with my invitation, which makes me so happy. I arrange to meet her the following day at the café I saw her at earlier that day. "Wonderful, so I'll see you tomorrow at 1:00 p.m."

"I look forward to it," Vanna says as she sets off running down the beach.

I make my way home, feeling a little excited. Maybe things are looking up. It will be nice to have someone to talk to other than Leo. I love Leo very much, but a girl needs her friends. Once I have settled Mark in bed, I make a cup of tea and get myself comfy on the sofa with a blanket. There's a new series on Netflix I have been wanting watch. But as soon as it starts, I get a sharp pain that shoots through my stomach.

Panicking, I clutch my tummy. "Please, no Not yet, my baby. It's too soon to meet you."

I feel our little one turn and see what I think is their bottom protrude through the front of my stomach. I stand to take a look at myself through the full-length mirror on the wall, turning from side to side and lifting my top to see the shape of my bump. It's dropped. I smile and rub my tummy excitedly, feeling calmer. The pains I have been experiencing must be our baby turning and getting ready for their arrival next month.

After watching two episodes, I'm falling asleep, so I take myself off to bed. I fall asleep as soon as my head hits the pillow.

At 5:00 a.m., I am woken by high-pitched screams.

Leo

I move the overgrown shrubs and vines that conceal the underground entrance to the Guerra property. After lifting the steel door and climbing down the first few steps on the ladders, I carefully close myself in, hardly making a sound. It's pitch-black until I reach the ground beneath me.

Dim lights illuminate my path as I walk through the tunnel. The stench almost makes me gag, but I focus on the path in front of me, avoiding puddles of shit and dead animals. It takes me around fifteen minutes to quickly walk the length of the tunnel. I'm relieved when I see the ladders leading to the opening in the grounds. It brings me out at a concealed hatch by the swimming pool. Once I have checked the coast is clear I climb out, brush my suit down, and tighten my tie.

Holding my gun at the ready, I move through the grounds, hiding myself as much as possible behind shrubbery and garden walls. It's quiet. Too quiet. I hope I'm not too late. As I get closer to the house, the ground is covered with bodies of Martelé men. Kicking their limbs as I pass to check that they are in fact dead, I carefully manoeuvre between the blood and guts staining the once white porcelain footpaths.

As I enter through the back door of the property, I instantly hear the sound of voices. The kitchen no longer looks like part of a home. Every surface is covered with weapons and ammunition. I put my handgun back in its holster at my back and pick up a loaded machine gun. Following the sound of the voices, I step carefully through to the front of the house. After checking each room I pass, I reach the room where the commotion is coming from.

Peering through the crack by the hinges in the door, I see Marco and Van tied to chairs to the left. Martelé men stand to the right. I'm furious to see my men being held hostage by Martelé on

Guerra soil. I plan my careful retaliation, but then lose my head when I hear the words of the Martelé.

"Here, today, you will witness the death of the last Guerra. After this moment, I do not want that name to ever be said again. The Guerra name dies with him."

I see red. My body burns and pulsates with fury. Without thinking, I fire the machine gun through the door in the direction of the Martelé. They return fire in my direction. Bullets shoot through the walls, narrowly missing my head. I step back, shielding myself behind a marble cabinet in the hallway. I return fire again, holding my arm up in their direction until their retaliation comes to an end.

Leaving it a moment, I wait in my retreat for any indication of survivors. I light a cigar and take a long drag to calm my nerves. When I don't hear a sound, I approach the door. Peering through the opening, I see the lifeless Martelé bodies on the floor. I'm relieved to see Marco and Van looking at each other in disbelief. A rush of exhilaration shoots through my body. It's a welcome euphoria I hadn't realised I had missed until now.

Entering through the doorway, I take another drag of my cigar, feeling smug as I watch the expressions on Van's and Marco's faces.

Van bursts into laughter. "What took you so long?"

Van was the one who called me and asked for help. I had guessed he had done this without Marco's knowledge. And from the look on Marco's face right now, I definitely guessed correctly.

"Aren't you supposed to be fucking dead?" Marco booms.

"Had to come and save your sorry ass, didn't I?" I reply as I untie Van, who is still finding the situation hilarious, unlike Marco, who is furious I have intervened.

"What have you fucking done! You died so you and your wife could live. Now you have just put another bounty on both your heads!"

He is pissing me off now. Does he think I don't know what I risked to come here? I stand in front of him, looking him in the eyes. "Marco. My sole purpose has always been to protect my family. You are my family. I wouldn't even be alive now if it wasn't for the many times you have saved my life. Now, don't ever question my judgement again."

As I release Marco from his restraints, he tries to stand up. But as he does, he falls. I just about support his heavy frame. When I look down, I see the reason for his unsteadiness. "Shit, look at the state of you."

Blood soaks his ankles and pools around his feet. Once I've sat him back down, I take a closer look. His heels have been shot. It's a mess. He will be lucky to walk again. Infuriated, I wish the

Martelé weren't dead so I could kill them again, much slower.

After instructing Van to arrange confidential emergency treatment with the best surgeon money can buy, I bandage Marco's wounds up the best I can. Van pulls the car as close to the front door as possible. I'm worried about Marco. He is in a bad way. He dozes in and out of consciousness as we carry him to the car. We need to get him medical attention soon, or we are going to lose him.

We get Marco to the medical centre in record time. The Guerra have their own private entrance, with minimal staff who are on our payroll.

Once Marco is in good hands, I ask Van to explain the Guerra's situation. "I want to know everything. Leave nothing out. From the moment I left three years ago until now."

The hours while Marco is in surgery pass by quickly. I pace up and down the room, listening to the turmoil the Guerra organisation has now become.

"The damage began when Mia disappeared," Van explains.

But he is wrong. The destruction started when I faked my own death. I left Marco on his own. He had no elders to guide him, no one on his level for support. Van is a number-one man, but he is not a Guerra. He does not share the same blood.

The situation is far worse than I first thought. The whole existence of the Guerra is at stake.

When Marco's surgery is complete, he is brought into the room with Van and me. The surgeon is pleased with how the operation went, the damage wasn't as severe as first expected.

"He needs rest and time to heal," the surgeon explains without making eye contact.

"Thank you, Doctor. Unfortunately that's easier said than done with this one," I reply as I look at my strong number one lying unconscious and helpless in his bed.

After telling me everything he knows, Van looks to me for guidance. "What's the plan, then, boss? Surely, we can expect a retaliation from the Martelé?"

Van is right. A retaliation will come. Although not just yet. They will have to appoint a new leader, which will take time, seeing as the next in the bloodline is only twelve years old. I explain this to Van. Although I'm speaking positivity and assertively, at this point, with me being *dead,* I don't see how the Guerra stand a chance.

"In the meantime, we need to build ourselves back up. Bigger and stronger than ever," I state, having no idea how we will achieve this.

Our attention is caught by the sound of

alarms. Marco sits bolt upright in bed, ripping the monitors from his chest.

Chapter Five

Katie

Mark's screams have me running to his bedroom. I find him soaked in sweat with his heart racing. "It's okay, little one. Mummy is here." I cradle him to my chest until he calms down.

"The monsters took me away," he cries, telling me about his nightmare.

Deciding we may as well stay up now, I take Mark downstairs and make him some milk while he watches his favourite television programme. While stood in the kitchen, I stare out of the window. It's still dark outside, and with the lights on inside I can see my reflection in the glass. I look scared and alone. Which I am. My thoughts go to Leo. I miss him terribly. I hope he is safe. I can't bear the thought of life without him. What would I do if he never came home? I'd be stuck here, on this island, with no friends or family. Yes, I would have my children, but what life would they have with only me? How could I look after them alone? Tears roll down my face. This was supposed to be our happily ever after. But right now, I've never been so unhappy.

The sound of Mark's laughter brings me out of my self-pity. *Pull it together Katie. It's just your hormones.* Everything is going to be fine. Leo will ring at 9:00, which will settle my nerves, and then I'm meeting Vanna for coffee. Maybe she and I will become friends, and this will be the start of us finally settling into a full life here.

After sitting by the phone for what seems like hours, 9:00 finally comes around, and it rings on the minute. Leo seems tense. He asks about Mark and me, but there's no warmth in his tone, and he seems very distracted. I ask when I should expect him home, but he avoids the question.

When the call ends, I'm more on edge then I was before it. But I have plenty to keep my mind busy. Mark and I potter about our grounds, tending to the vineyard, feeding the animals, and playing our usual game of hide-and-seek. At 11:00 a.m., I put Mark down for a nap while I get showered and ready to meet Vanna.

Mark and I arrive at the café early. I want to get our usual table and settle Mark with the picnic I have brought him to keep him occupied. From our carefully selected table, I see Vanna approaching. She looks amazing. Her perfect hourglass figure is hugged by a simple white dress. As she walks, her dark hair flows in the light breeze. She smiles at the waiter who greets her, and her green eyes sparkle in the sunlight. Vanna is one of those women who will rarely look anything but stunning every day of the year. *Bitch,* I think to myself jokingly as I sit up a little bit straighter, feeling self-conscious.

"Vanna, over here." I wave, thankful that she has turned up. I did have my doubts. "I'm so pleased you came."

"Katie, of course, I've been looking forward to it. And how's Mark? No more running off from your mummy, I hope?"

Mark doesn't make a sound, just stares at Vanna wide-eyed and open-mouthed, mesmerised by the dark-haired beauty that has joined us.

"No, thank goodness, although I have been keeping him on a tight leash since his last getaway. Thank you again for that."

"Don't worry. You definitely have your hands full—and another one on the way." Vanna gestures towards my baby bump. "Do you know what you're having?"

"No, we are leaving it as a surprise." I rub my belly, feeling excited to know what our next child will be.

There's a break in our conversation as Vanna takes out her compact mirror and inconspicuously scans the café around us. To others this would simply look like she is checking that the application of her lipstick is still intact. But I am married to the last leader of the Guerra. I notice everything. Her action puts me on guard at first. Many thoughts pop into my mind. Is she a spy? Has she been sent here to find us? But something in my gut tells me I can trust her.

"There are twelve people currently in the café, not including us." I lean in towards her to speak quietly. "One family of four, two couples, two waiters, and two kitchen staff. I recognise all the staff, apart from one guy in the kitchen. And judging by the obscenities I've heard coming from the usual chef, he's new and isn't very good."

Vanna arches one of her perfectly sculptured brows at what I've revealed about myself through that assessment.

I sit back comfortably in my chair and hope my gut instincts are right.

Vanna also relaxes and laughs. "I think we are going to get on very well, Katie."

And we do. We both have lunch and talk nonstop for two full hours. Not about anything personal, we both are very careful about that, but we discuss the eccentric characters who live on the island. Our favourite pastimes and places to go to see the most beautiful views. The only reason we end our conversation is Mark has gotten bored of the many snacks and toys I have given him.

As we leave the café, we say our goodbyes.

"Please let's do this again soon, Katie."

"Definitely, I'd love that. How about—" My reply is cut off by a sharp pain that shoots through my stomach. Suddenly I feel hot, and sick.

"Katie? Are you okay?"

Vanna puts her arm around me just as another pain explodes, making me double over. I reach out desperately to support myself with Mark's pushchair.

"Come back inside. Let's sit you down." Vanna tries to usher me back inside the café, but Mark is screaming his head off, wanting to get going.

"No, I'm okay, thank you," I lie, standing up and breathing through the pain. "I just need to get home." I'm sure the pain will ease off just like it has the past few days. It's probably just Braxton Hicks. I remember getting them before I had Mark, although I don't remember them being this painful.

"All right, if you're sure. But let me walk you home."

"Okay, thank you."

By the time we get back to our house, the pains are getting worse and more frequent. I'm starting to panic, as I think I might be in labour.

44

"Shout for your husband, and then I'll leave you, but I really think you should go to the hospital." Vanna helps me get Mark inside the house.

"My husband isn't here." I cry as the next contraction hits.

"Where is he? Can you ring him?"

"No, I don't know his number." I can hardly speak, my breathing is so erratic.

"Is there anyone I can call for you? Someone to look after Mark?" Vanna takes her phone out of her bag.

It's the first time in years I've seen a mobile phone up close. Leo got rid of ours when we left Italy, and we've never needed one since. My body starts to shake. I feel dizzy and can't see clearly. Sweat drips from my eyebrows into my eyes.

"No, I have no one."

Vanna looks at me with sympathy and understanding. "Okay, don't worry. I will call my husband now. He will take us to the hospital. Tell me where your things are, and I'll take care of you and Mark."

"Thank you," I sob, grateful that she is here.

"Everything is going to be fine. Just sit here and rest."

Vanna quickly packs a bag for Mark with

toys, a change of clothes, and refreshments. She then gets my hospital bag, which I've already packed. As soon as she is done, there's a knock at the door.

"My husband is here. Let me get Mark into the car, and then I'll come back and help you."

I do as Vanna says, having no other option than to let a woman I have just met, and a stranger, take my little boy out of my house. Sure enough, a moment later, Vanna returns and helps me lock up the house and get into the car.

"In cosa ti sei cacciata ora?" *What have you gotten yourself into now?* Vanna's husband says to her quietly as he pulls the car into the road.

"Katie speaks Italian, my love."

"Ah, my apologies, Katie. I see you're having a baby. Congratulations."

As I'm unable to reply or even lift my head to look at him, Vanna speaks for me. "Don't talk. Just drive."

The hospital is only five minutes away. Vanna helps me out of the car and into the maternity unit. Her husband takes Mark to the hospital café to get an ice cream. Thankfully Mark has taken to him. I try not to let myself think about the danger he could be in. I wish Leo were here. Stepping into the modern reception area, I'm grateful to see a friendly looking nurse.

"Oh, love, you look like you need some help. Here, take a seat, and I'll take you through to the ward."

Vanna lets go of my arm once I'm sat in the wheelchair. She follows behind us with my bag. The smell of clinical products mixed with hospital food, the shouts of pain from women in labour, blended with beeping from medical equipment— the sensory overload is astonishing as I'm taken into a private room. I'm scared. I shouldn't be doing this alone. The nurse helps me stand from the wheelchair. As I go to sit on the bed, an almighty pain is followed by a gush between my legs.

"Oh, I'm sorry," I apologise, knowing I have just ruined the crisp white sheets.

"Don't worry, dear, that will just be your waters breaking," the nurse reassures me. Until she looks down at the floor and then back to me with an expression that no longer puts me at ease.

I then smell the distinctive pungent, metallic stench. As I look down, my legs turn to jelly at the sight. Crimson blood soaks my legs and feet. A pool of blood gradually grows larger as it continues to run down my legs.

"Let's get you onto the bed."

The room spins in multiple colours as I lie facing the ceiling. More people enter the room. I know they are speaking to me, as I hear my name, but I'm unable to respond. A tingling sensation, almost like pins and needles, runs down my limbs to my fingers and toes. The colours in my vision become darker, blending into one. The room disappears. Darkness takes over.

Leo

After having spent all night going through police reports and CCTV, I find myself waking up in my old—now Marco's—office chair. It's a familiar surrounding and not the first time I have fallen asleep here. The morning sun shines through the open curtains. When I look at my watch and realise the time, I quickly open the safe and retrieve the radio phone. While I wait for Katie to answer, I hear voices outside. Knowing I need to leave before I am seen, I put the phone into my pocket. Katie hasn't answered. It is an hour later there. Katie has probably gotten tired of waiting for my call and taken Mark out to see the animals. Smiling, I think of his impatient tantrums of a morning because he wants to go and see his goats, Upsy and Daisy.

I make my escape unseen and arrive at the hospital to explain my discovery to Van and then Marco.

"They switched clothes," Marco says in

disbelief as I show him my findings. It transpires that the woman who was killed in this accident wasn't Mia. Van's sister and Marco's woman could in fact still be alive.

When Katie and I faked our own deaths and fled Italy, Marco took over as leader of the Guerra. Marco, who I thought could never love a woman, had his heart stolen by Mia Alboni, the daughter of my father's number one. I had noticed their "friends with benefits" arrangement before I left, but I never thought it would have transformed into what it did. It seems Mia stole his heart over the years. Unfortunately, about six months ago, Mia went to London to attend a marketing campaign for her beauty brand. On the evening of the event, Mia was killed. Although Marco and Van never fully understood what happened, they knew the Martelé were behind it. Upon finding out the Martelé were responsible, Marco retaliated without thinking, trying to catch them off guard on their turf. The Martelé saw him coming. Marco left barely alive, having started the biggest war our organisation has ever seen. When Van explained all these past events to me in the hospital, something just didn't fit into place. The Martelé are far from discreet in their execution of tasks, but a car ploughing into Mia and her friends while they were on the doorstep of a busy bar seemed too messy, even for them.

After watching the CCTV of the night in

question, I am one hundred percent sure the woman killed in that video was not Mia.

The decision is made to go to London. Marco is in no fit state, but that doesn't stop him. And I don't' blame him. If this were Katie, I would do the same. Katie. I ring her again before I board the jet. Again, there is no answer. Although concerned, I put it to the back of my mind. The sooner we get to the bottom of what happened to Mia, the sooner I can get back to my family.

On the flight over, we gather all the information we can. We speak to our contacts in England and go over additional police reports from that night. Having found the name of the only survivor of the accident, it doesn't take long for us to find an address.

I drive Van and Marco to the location. The local police, to whom we've explained our findings, also meet us there. Unfortunately, this isn't Italy, and it can be, let's say, an inconvenience to deal with situations the Guerra way, much to Marco's disappointment. The police do, however, let Marco enter the house alone. While I wait, I ring Katie again. No answer. The feeling in my gut I have been suppressing resurfaces. She's in trouble. I need to get to her immediately.

Marco leaves the house not having found Mia, but he has been told she is at a nearby hospital. After dropping Van and Marco off there,

I make my way to the airfield. Taking the Guerra jet to the island is a very risky move. This could not only make the Martelé aware I am still alive, but it could also lead them to my location. Unfortunately, I have no choice. I need to get to my family as soon as possible.

During the flight, I continuously ring the phone in my kitchen. Each time it rings out, the more frustrated and angry I become. I feel helpless and infuriated with myself for having left the most important people in the world to me. I left them alone. I left my heavily pregnant, precious wife on an island with no one she could turn to for help. The thought of what may have happened to them has me throwing up in the toilet. Maybe I haven't been as careful as I had thought. The Martelé may have already found her. I heave until my stomach is empty and my veins bulge through my skin.

After washing my hands and splashing my face with water, I stare at my reflection in the bathroom mirror. A stern expression with furrowed brows covers my face. It's a look I haven't been used to since moving to the island. Fury builds inside of me, and I roar out in anger. I grip the side of the sink I am leaning on and rip it from the wall. Shouting again, I throw the sink out of the bathroom into the cabin lounge of the aircraft. A piercing alarm sounds snaping me out of my outburst. As I walk out of the bathroom, one of the crew members has entered, no doubt to determine the course of the noise.

"Get the fuck out! You were instructed to under no circumstances to enter this part of the plane!" I throw the tap, which is still in my hand, in her direction.

The woman stands for a moment, staring at me in disbelief. I recognise her as one of the usual Guerra jet cabin crew. No doubt she also recognises me. Shit.

"I'm so sorry, Mr Guerra. I... I... won't say a word. I'm so sorry," she apologises, looking like she is about to cry as she exits, closing the door behind her.

Sitting down in the nearest chair, I put my head in my hands. "Oh, Katie, where are you? Please be safe."

I then go through all the different possibilities of what could have happened to Katie and Mark. Number one, which I dismiss instantly due to not being able to comprehend the outcome, is that the Martelé have found out their location and they are either already dead or being kept until they have me. I move on to number two, which seems the mostly likely. Something has happened to Mark that has resulted in them not being able to be at home. Mark is a little rascal and always up to mischief. He has no awareness of danger. He has probably fallen and broken his arm or injured himself in some way, and they are both at the hospital. Number three, Katie has gone deaf and cannot hear the phone. Or number four, something is wrong with Katie and the baby.

I'm relieved when I feel the jet starting to descend.

There's a car waiting for me when I leave the plane. It takes me straight to our house.

"Kat-er-een!" I shout as I rush through each room, searching for my wife and child.

I'm not surprised to find every room empty, but I had hoped they would be here. Taking in the scene in each room, I look for signs of a disturbance. All the doors are locked, and there's no sign of a struggle, which puts me at ease—a little. When I enter our bedroom, I notice an empty space next to Katie's dressing table. Her hospital bag—it's gone.

I rush back down the stairs, grab my car keys, and exit the house. I start the car, then immediately pull out of our driveway without looking. Thankfully there is nothing on the roads, and I arrive at the hospital in under five minutes. I abandon my car outside the entrance and then run through the doors and up to the reception.

"Where is my wife?" I demand. Until I remember where I am. "I'm sorry. I'm looking for Katie Smith. I'm Mr Smith, her husband."

"That's okay, Mr Smith. Let me just check the computer."

The way I'm tapping the desk impatiently with my finger has the receptionist muttering something under her breath. Then she says, "Okay. Your wife is on M block, room one. But I must tell you, Mr…"

She continues speak to me, but I don't wait. I run through the long hospital hallways, following the red arrows that direct me to M block.

"Room one?" I ask one of the nurses when I arrive.

She points at a door to the side of me. As I push the door open, she shouts, "Sir, wait!"

But I don't. I walk straight into a situation that takes all the air out of my lungs. It's like an elephant is stood on my chest. A familiar heart-wrenching pain rips through my soul. No. This cannot be true. It must be my imagination playing tricks on me. I do not believe the sight in front of me.

Chapter Six

Katie

It's quiet and dark. Oh, what's that? A tiny white light appears in front of me. When I try to reach out and touch it, nothing happens. I look down, but I don't see my body. No arms or legs or body parts. Just dark emptiness. Mark suddenly comes into my mind. As the longing for my son grows within me, the white light grows bigger. An image of his face has me feeling warmer. The light now fills my vision. It then reappears and disappears repeatedly over and over until I finally realise, I'm blinking. Once I open my eyes wide, they begin to focus. It's blurry, but I can see.

"Welcome back, Katie."

The voice at my side makes me jump.

"It's okay. Lie back down. I'm Paula, your nurse. You're in hospital, but we are taking good care of you."

I recognise her to be the friendly nurse I met on my arrival.

"My son Mark? And my baby?" I cradle my stomach in my arms. It feels empty. "Where are my babies?" I cry.

"Sshh, hey, don't worry. They are both absolutely fine." The nurse takes my hand in hers and lightly squeezes. "Mark is with your friends. They have taken him to the family room. And your other little boy is here, right beside you." The nurse lets go of my hand and pushes a tiny Perspex cot towards me.

"It's a boy." My heart melts at the first sight of my son. For months, I have tried to imagine what he would look like. I thought he would look like Mark did as a newborn. But he looks different. He's the image of his dad, like Mark is, but in a different way. "Can I hold him?"

"Of course. Here, let me sit you up a little more and put a pillow under your arm to support you. There, how's that?" the nurse asks as she places my newborn son in my arms.

"Perfect. Thank you." My heart pumps hard with love for my child. He makes a little murmuring sound as he wriggles to get comfy. "Is he okay?" I ask, remembering he is a month early.

"He is absolutely fine. He has been checked over by the doctor. Ten fingers and ten toes." The nurse laughs. "But you, young lady, gave us quite a scare. The baby's placenta had started to detach from your uterus wall. We got baby here out just in time, but you suffered severe blood loss, causing cardiac arrest. Fortunately, the team were able to get you heart going again. The doctor will go over everything in more detail. You just rest with your little one."

Feeling very overwhelmed but incredibly grateful to be here, I stare at my baby. Leo will be devasted he has missed this. He will be beside himself with me not being there to answer his calls. He is due back anytime. He did say it would only be two to three days. We are now into the early hours of day three.

"Paula."

The friendly nurse is instantly at my bedside. "Yes?"

"Would you mind asking Vanna if she would bring Mark to see me, please? I would really like to see him, and I think it's time for him to meet his little brother."

"Of course. I will go and get them from the family room. I'm sure they'll all be pleased to see you awake. Everyone has been very worried about you. Oh, have you got a name for the little one yet?"

"Yes, we do. My husband and I had decided on a name for both a boy and girl. The boy's name is Alex, after his late brother. But I will have to check with my husband when he arrives."

"Alex, lovely." The nurse gently strokes my son's head. "Right, I will go and get his big brother. Back in minute."

The nurse leaves us, and I whisper, "Welcome to the world. Your daddy and I are going to love you so much, and you have got the best big brother."

I hope Leo is still happy with the name choice. I better wait to confirm it with him before telling anyone else. But I know how much his brother meant to him, so I'm sure he will still feel the same about the name. Leo always felt guilty about Alex's death. He wasn't around when he was killed. Leo was in England, looking for me. I'm glad Leo wasn't there, though, as I know Leo would have done anything to protect his brother. He would have ended up dead too. Alex had unknowingly fallen in love with the daughter of the Martelé boss. Leo's father, who was the head of the Guerra at the time, had tried to make a truce between the two organisations. Which seemed to have been accepted at first. But it was all a trap to gain the Guerra trust and hit them when they least expected. Leo is sure Alex's girlfriend was in on the deceit. But soon after, she committed suicide.

I hear Mark shouting down the hallway. The nurse opens the door. She comes in, holding Mark's hand.

"Now, Mark, remember what I said. Mummy

is very tired, and your new brother is very small, so we need to be very careful, okay?"

"Okay," Mark repeats. His face is a picture as the nurse lifts him onto the bed bedside me. He doesn't take his eyes off Alex.

"Hey, baby." Wrapping my free arm around Mark, I pull him towards me and kiss his head, breathing in his scent. "This is your brother."

"Hello, baby brother," Mark says, speaking so softly.

"He loves you so much."

Mark beams with pride, looking from me to his younger sibling.

"Katie, I'm so pleased you are all right," Vanna says as she enters the room, followed by her husband.

Her tall, dark, and very handsome husband. I can't take my eyes off him. He has a powerful presence that fills the room. If I didn't know any better, I'd say he was a Guerra.

Noise outside my room pulls me away from my stare. Heavy footsteps and a nurse shouting has everyone turning to the door. It swings open, and my breath catches in relief and happiness. "Leo."

He is a thing of beauty. He stands powerfully. His crisp suit is a little dishevelled, and his hair is far from the immaculate slicked-back style it was when he left. But he has never looked so handsome. Butterflies flutter in my stomach at the reminder of when we first got to together in Italy. It was far from ideal, but it is our story, and I wouldn't change it for the world. After a moment of Leo being stuck to the spot, I realise he hasn't looked at me or our sons yet. He looks like he has seen a ghost. When I look along his line of vision, I see Vanna's husband wearing the same disturbed expression.

"Alex," Leo croaks.

The emotions running through me have my head spinning and my eyes blurring. My limbs start to feel heavy, and I'm worried I might drop my son.

"Paula, please," I manage to muster through the shallow breaths I can't help but take.

Paula quickly comes to my aid and takes my baby from my arms and then lifts Mark from the bed as well. Leo's eyes eventually land on me. But his face disappears into darkness.

Just before I lose consciousness, I hear Leo boom through the room, "Get out! Get the hell out!"

Leo

The air is sucked from my lungs as watch my wife lose consciousness.

"Get out! Get the hell out!" I bellow at my dead brother. My mind is in overdrive, but my priority is my wife.

"What's wrong with her? You need to help her," I demand of the nurse, who is working quickly, checking monitors and changing a drip.

"Why don't you take your boys to the family room, and I'll send a doctor to come and speak to you."

"No, I'm staying here." My outbursts and the seriousness of the situation have Mark screaming and clinging on to my leg.

"Please, sir. Take your boys. Your wife is in good hands."

Three more medical staff enter the room. One of them helps me push the tiny cot my newborn son has been placed in into the family room. I feel helpless. I don't do well with not being in control. But for now, the best thing I can do is take care of my boys.

A nurse brings some milk, a blanket, and pillows for Mark, and he is soon asleep on a sofa beside me. Then she passes me some formula and the baby bag.

"Here." The nurse places my newborn son in my arms. "He's ready for a feed and no doubt a nappy change. If you need a hand or if there's anything you need, just give me a shout. I'm right outside the door."

As I hold him in my arms, I study his little face. His eyes are closed, but his brow is creased with a frown. His arms stretch out, and I place my index finger in his wrinkly hand. He squeezes it tightly and opens his eyes.

"Hello, little one. I am your papa." And in that moment, our unbreakable bond is made. My protective mode is activated. I feel a wave of guilt for not being here when he was born and for leaving my wife alone in what has she been through. I wasn't there to protect her. I vow never to leave their sides again. As my youngest son begins to stir, I place his bottle between his lips. Once he tastes the milk, he feeds hungrily. While I appreciate these first moments with my son, I cannot help but think of my wife. While I cannot call myself a religious man, I turn to the god of the universe, praying for my wife to live.

Once feeding time is over and I have winded and changed my son, my impatience gets the better of me. As I open the door of the family room, I'm met with a red-haired man I presume is a doctor, given his attire.

"Mr Smith? Is it?" the doctor asks, rereading the notes he has in his hand. As no, I do not look like a Mr Smith.

When we relocated, we decided to keep our first names, as it would get too confusing, but we had to change our last name. So, for all intents and purposes, I am Mr Smith.

"Correct. How is my wife?"

"She is comfortable and conscious. And demanding to see you."

Of course she is.

"Before you go to her, I would just like to go through her past medical history. Please take a seat." The doctor gestures to the chair I was sitting on a moment ago.

"No, I'll stand. Please continue."

"As you wish. Has your wife ever suffered with any cardiological issues?"

"No."

"Does she have any previous diagnoses or illnesses?"

"No."

The doctor checks his notes.

"What has happened to my wife, Doctor?"

"Your wife suffered a cardiac arrest. Thankfully she was in the hospital when this occurred. If this have occurred outside a medical facility, I'm afraid your wife would not have had the same outcome."

The statement has a lump building in my throat.

"You baby's placenta detached from your wife's womb. This caused severe internal bleeding, in turn creating traumatic stress on your wife's body, which then caused the cardiac arrest."

At this point, I do sit down. I place my baby in his crib then put my head in my hands. I rub my face, trying to process. I could have lost my wife. *My wife.* I should have been here to protect my family. If she had died, so would I.

"So far your wife seems to be recovering well."

"Seems to be?" I demand, not liking how that was put.

"Yes. A cardiac arrest is very serious and can have many different long-term effects. Your wife may have some of them or none at all, but it is too early to tell at the moment. We will be keeping a close eye on her and carrying out more tests."

"What kind of long-term effects?"

"It's a lack of oxygen to the brain during a cardiac arrest that can sometimes cause further complications. Things like personality changes, problems with memory, feeling tired, dizziness or balance issues. Problems with speech and language, as well as irreversible damage to the heart."

"Am I going to lose my wife?"

"As I said, Mr Smith, your wife is recovering well at this early stage. She is young and otherwise healthy. But she is going to need a lot of care, especially with a newborn. Her rehabilitation must be slow and gentle. No unnecessary stress."

"She won't lift a finger." I stand, needing to be near my world.

"Let me take you to her. I'll get the nurse to come and take care of your sons."

Before entering her room, I take a deep breath to compose myself, cracking my neck to release some tension. Gently, I open the door and find her sleeping. Her blonde hair is fanned across her pillow. She looks like an angel in the crisp white sheets. A very pale, frail-looking angel. The difference in her appearance in just a few days is painful.

The nurse notices me standing at the door. "Come on in, love. Here, have a seat next to her." The nurse pulls a chair up beside the bed.

Taking a seat beside her, I gently take hold of her bruised hand. She feels cold.

"I'll give you some privacy. But if you need anything, just press that orange button." She points to a remote control attached to Katie's bed.

To warm her hand, I place my other one over top. Gently, I kiss the tips of her fingers.

"Leo?" Katie begins to stir. Her voice quiet and pained.

"Yes, it's me, Kat-er-een. I'm here. You just rest."

"I've missed you so much. I've been so scared." A little sob leaves her lips.

Guilt ripples through me. "I'm here now, and I'll never leave you again."

"I couldn't get hold of you. I thought something had happened to you."

"Hey. Just relax. Everything is fine. I'm okay, the boys are okay, and you're okay. I'm going to take care of you all."

"Ti amo." *I love you*.

"Ti amo, Kat-er-een." *I love you*.

While Katie continues to doze, I worry about how I am going to care for her and how I am going to care for my two young sons. Am I enough? Katie is a fantastic mother. She makes everything seem effortless. Although this life may seem more relaxed than our previous one, Katie does everything in our home single-handedly. Obviously, I tend to the vineyard and help out with the animals. But the household chores and day-to-day running of our home is all Katie. I always offer to help, but she refuses, enjoying being the caring mother taking care of her family.

Back in Italy, we had help. A cleaner, a chef,

a housekeeper, a gardener. We also had family and friends. Here we have no one.

Alex's face appears in my mind. He is alive. Anger builds inside of me. The pain and guilt I have suffered for years, blaming myself for his death, when all this time he was alive. And with her. A Martelé. The pain her family has caused. How could he be with such evil?

So many questions. The need for so many answers. Did he know we were here? Is she still working with the Martelé? My protective instincts flare. I need to protect my family. Suddenly I feel very vulnerable. Defenceless. There is only so much I can do to protect the three most precious people in the world. We need security. But there's nothing like that here. And who would I trust to look after them who could I trust to die for my loved ones? Nobody here. They're all back in Italy. If word has gotten back to the Martelé that I am alive, they could already be on their way. They may already be here. And one of them *is*. The distance between myself and my sons feels like a shot in my heart. We all need to be together. Quietly slipping out of Katie's room, I return the family room. During the short walk, I hear my name being called.

"Leo."

Instantly recognising his voice, I stop in my tracks, turning to see my brother with the Martelé woman.

"How's Katie?"

"Do not dare talk about my wife. Leave before I kill you myself." Turning I continue to my sons.

"Leo, please," the Martelé begs.

"And you. Stay away from my wife and children."

"Do not disrespect my wife!" Alex booms.

"Please, it's fine. He's upset. Let's just go." She takes hold of his arm, trying to pull him away.

"Yes, listen to your wife, Alex." Alex. The name I treasured, the name we were planning on calling our new son now feels tainted.

"Five minutes, Leo. And then you never have to see us again."

Taking a deep breath while cracking my neck, I consider his request. The safety of my family is my main concern. "You have one minute."

Alexs follows me into the family room. I dismiss the nurse, and thankfully my sons are safe and still sound asleep.

"Is my family safe?" I ask as soon as the nurse closes the door.

Alex looks at me quizzically.

"She is Martelé. Are my wife and children safe?"

"Vanna is no longer a Martelé."

"Does anyone know we are here?"

"Why would anyone know you are here?"

"Just answer the question."

Alex rubs his jaw with his right hand. A frown mirroring mine crosses his forehead. "Look. I have no idea what is going on with you or where you have been. The suit you are wearing has me worried." He sighs and shakes his head a little. "But I have connections at the airbase and all the ports on the island. They keep me informed with any new arrivals or suspicious activity. Other than you and a stowaway who left for three days and returned on a jet, there haven't been any further updates."

The fact that he knows I left doesn't fill me with confidence. But for now, the fact my family isn't in any immediate danger puts me at ease slightly. "Your minute is up."

Before Alex can protest, Mark wakes. "Papa?"

"I'm here, son." Taking him in my arms, I sit down with him on my lap.

"I'll leave you for now. But I will see you again soon."

I don't answer. A response doesn't come to

mind. I hear them both leave, closing the door behind them. My feelings on the situation make me feel like punching a wall. After gathering up my boys' belongings, I lift Mark with one arm and push the cot with my youngest son back into Katie's room.

The nurse sets up bed in the corner of the room, and for the next few days, we spend all our time together within those four walls, apart from me nipping home to feed the animals and pick up necessities. Katie, like the strong, amazing woman she is, has been gaining strength each day. She is even breast feeding now, which the nurse says is fantastic after everything she has been through. Mark has been getting lots of attention from the nurses, and I'm enjoying being around my family safe in our bubble.

Until today. When Alex returns and drops a bombshell.

Chapter Seven

Katie

Watching my husband play with our eldest son makes my heart burst with love. Lying in my bed, cradling our sleeping youngest—who we still haven't officially named yet, and I'm not sure how to bring it up, given the *Alex* revelation—makes me appreciate so many things. It's scary to think that I almost died a few days ago. I almost lost this bundle of joy in my arms. I almost left Mark without a mother and Leo without a wife. It's strange how being a parent makes you feel so differently about life. Before children, my fear of dying was for myself. Now when I think about dying, my worst fear is leaving my children without a mother. Feeling their pain of losing a parent. A pain I hope they never have to face until they are much, much older.

It's been a few days now since we found out that Leo's brother Alex is in fact alive and well. Leo hasn't wanted to discuss it, so I haven't pushed. At first I was shocked, but now that I've thought about it, it's not that shocking. We have done exactly the same thing. Considering the world that Leo and Alex have come from, it's not that much of a surprise. I'm actually excited about what the future will hold.

"Leo, we really need to decide on a name."

"Not yet."

"Yes, yet. He's three days old now. We need to talk about this.

"You think of something, then."

"No, Leo. This not how we name one of the most precious things in the world. We both decided on Alex, and that's what I think we should stick with."

Leo leaves Mark playing happily with a jigsaw and comes to stand beside me.

Leo stumbles over his words. "I-I can't…."

"Look, I know you've just had the shock of your life, but you're thinking about this all wrong. It's a wonderful thing that your brother is alive."

Leo's face grows angry, his expression hurt. He puts his hands at my sides on the bed and leans in. He speaks quietly, but his voice is laced with annoyance. "A good thing? My brother has lied to me for all these years. He caused me horrendous pain. Made me blame myself. Is that a good thing?"

"He has only done what we have. Other than

Marco and your mother, the rest of our friends and family think we are dead."

My breath catches when I think of the pain I have caused my parents.

When we first left, Leo asked if I wanted them to know. But the risk of them knowing was too high. It would put them in danger. My mother has a big mouth and would have definitely told someone. If they had seemed at all suspicious in their grief, the Martelé would have come after them, tortured them until they told them the truth. I couldn't bear that. I had to protect them.

"You made *me* do this, Leo. I had no choice in the matter. You left me with no option but to put my parents through the worst pain imaginable."

Leo stands, his face softening. Taking my hand in his. he speaks more calmly, but matter-of-factly.

"I'm sorry. If there had been any other way, we would have done it differently. But we had no choice. There was no other option."

Squeezing his hand back, I answer, "Exactly. So don't you think Alex had no other option either? Do you think that *he* made this decision lightly?"

Leo's eyes leave mine, and I can see him processing my words.

"You need to speak to him."

Leo sighs. "I need to take care of you."

"And you are. But sorting this out will stop me from worrying. Please?"

There's a little tap at the door, followed by the nurse entering. "You have visitors. Is it okay for them to come in?"

Vanna's head pops over the nurse's shoulder.

I look at Leo pleadingly.

He nods. "Yeah, sure. Send them in."

Vanna rushes over to my side. But Alex stays in the doorway.

"Can I have a word?" Alex gestures for Leo to follow him from the room.

At first, I think he is going to decline, but he kisses my forehead and promises to be back soon. Once they both leave, I turn my attention to Vanna.

Her face full of smiles and emotion as she looks at my son in my arms. She strokes the top of his head. "He's absolutely gorgeous."

"Thank you." I beam.

"And how are you?" Vanna pulls up a chair at the side of me and takes a seat.

"I'm fine. A little tired but just grateful to be here. Thank you so much for everything you have done for us, Vanna. I don't dare think what might have happened if you weren't around."

"Don't mention it. We've been so worried about you all. We are just glad you are okay."

There's a silence for a few moments, and I'm sure Vanna is thinking the same thing I am. So I decide to break the ice.

"It seems you are my sister-in-law. How's Alex taken the revelation?" I ask and then wonder whether he knew we were here.

"Well, he wouldn't speak to me about it at first. He needed to get his head around it, I suppose."

Sounds familiar.

"But we had a long talk last night, and I think he is doing better. Today he seems different. Like a fire has been ignited in him. One I haven't seen in years."

"So, you had no idea we were living here?"

"No. But we have a theory. Who arranged for you to come here?"

"Well, Leo, Marco, and Maria, Leo's mum."

Vanna smiles. "Maria. She is the one who helped us come here."

Wow. A million things run through my mind. Flashbacks of our wedding day. The explosions. Saying goodbye to Maria and Marco and getting into the boat. She planned this. She sent her only sons away. She saved them both. She knew they would find each other.

"I can't get my head around it all," I admit.

"It's definitely a story to tell the grandchildren." Vanna smiles.

"Here, would you like to hold him?"

"Love to." Vanna beams as I pass her my son. "Have you named him yet? I see his wrist band still says Baby Smith."

"Not officially. We have a name, but we are keeping it to ourselves for now. I'm sure we will be ready to share it soon."

Leo

"We need to talk." Alex's tone is matter-of-fact as I follow him out of Katie's room and down the hallway.

"Yes, I have a lot of questions."

"They will have to wait. We have an issue." Alex opens a door and looks inside. "In here." He beckons me into the empty storage room.

"What issue?" My adrenaline picks up, and I know I am not going to like what comes next.

"My contact at the airbase phoned me this morning. They found an unarranged stowaway in the todays cargo plane."

"Where are they?"

"Being detained until I arrive."

"I'll come with you."

"There's no doubt you *will* be coming with me. He is demanding to speak to Leo Guerra."

My blood runs cold. "Who is it?"

"How the fuck should I know? We will go now and find out. And on the way, you can justify this shit show."

Once we are alone in the car, I begin to talk. At first, Alex doesn't say much as I explain recent events He nods and cracks his neck, taking in the information. Mid-sentence, he cuts me off.

"Why the fuck did you have the phone in the first place?" he groans, rubbing his forehead.

"In case of emergencies such as this."

"You were supposed to be dead. Dead people are not resurrected when there is a crisis, Leo. They stay dead."

"I couldn't leave my family without knowing they were safe. I knew if that phone never rang, everything back home was in order. It meant I could get on with enjoying my life without feeling guilty for being happy." I turn to look at the side of my brother's face. "I guess that's how we differ, you and me. I still cared."

Fury builds in Alex's face. He doesn't speak,

so I continue. "You left your eighteen-year-old brother, who was never trained or brought up to be a leader, to deal with the mess you left. To stand on the front line of the Guerra. I blamed myself for your death."

Alex bangs his fists against the steering wheel. "Do not talk to me about guilt. You have no idea what I have felt. How hard it was to leave you."

I laugh. "You didn't think twice about me. All you thought about was yourself."

Alex abruptly swerves and pulls into the side of the road. The force of the brakes throws me forward.

"Shit!" I hold the dashboard to prevent myself from flying through the window. Probably should have fastened my seat belt.

"Did you even think about how convenient it was that we died when you were out of the country?" Alex grabs my shirt at the neck and pulls me to towards him.

I don't fight. I stare into his eyes, which are full of rage and emotion.

"Everything was planned so you wouldn't be anywhere near us. You would be safe. The Martelé wanted me dead. But they couldn't get to me. They wanted to hurt me. I had taken one of theirs. Vanna. So, they wanted to take one of mine." He presses his forehead firmly into mine before throwing me back into my seat.

Lost for words, I stare out of the window beside me. He did this to protect me.

"Don't you dare say I didn't care. The only way we differ is, I wasn't stupid enough to have a phone. And I wasn't stupid enough to go back."

After a moment or two, Alex puts the car in Drive and sets off again. "Now let's go and sort your mess out."

When the cars pulls to a stop at the airbase, Alex turns to me. "How did the Guerra get in such turmoil? It's unimaginable. I can't get my head around it. Marco is solid."

Having no explanation, I shake my head and sigh.

We are met at the car by Alex's contact, who leads us into an underground hangar. Two combat aircrafts stand pristine, men working underneath them.

"Has the detainee said anything since he arrived?" I ask the short bald man as he leads us through a door into a hallway.

"No. He refuses to speak to anyone. Just asks to see a Leo Guerra. So unless you are the man in question—" He looks to me. "—I doubt he will say a word." He then stops outside another door. "He's in here. The transport is ready for his departure whenever you are ready, Alex."

Alex nods, and the bald man leaves.

As I'm about to open the door, Alex stops me with a hand on my shoulder. "I'll do the talking. We find out who he is, who sent him, and if anyone else is with him. Then we escort him off the island and dispose of him."

Now is not the time for a battle of egos with my brother, so I shrug his hand off my shoulder and enter the room.

I'm surprised to see who is restrained to the chair in front of me.

Chapter Eight

Leo

"Van. What the fuck?"

"Boss." Van has a slight smirk on his face. He is obviously pleased to see me.

I, on the other hand, am not pleased to see him.

"Why are you here Van?"

"Van Alboni?" Alex questions. "What the hell is going on? This isn't some holiday camp that allows visitors. Why the fuck are you here?"

Van looks towards Alex. "Alex Guerra. Well, kill me now." Van laughs.

Alex lunges towards Van.

Quickly intervening, I pull him away before he does any damage.

"Do you think this is some kind of joke?" Alex demands.

Van loses the amused expression but doesn't

answer. He just stares at Alex. Van is a ruthless killer. He's very well built and uses every muscle to his advantage. Personality-wise, he is a little immature and can often lack common sense. But he makes up for that with his sharp sniper aim, his ability to kill someone with his bare hands, and his undetectable talent of killing a room full of people without making a sound.

"Boss." Van turns his attention to me, ignoring Alex. "Sorry for the unannounced intrusion, but I have been ringing the radio phone, and there has been no answer."

Alex huffs behind me at the mention of the phone.

"There has been word amongst the Martelé that you are in fact alive."

My gut churns with dread. My family are in danger.

"Do they know where I am?"

"As of yet, I don't think so. But they are getting close. Put it this way—Marco doesn't know I am here. I managed to find you."

I pace the room, thinking of my options. We could leave the island and go somewhere else. But if the Martelé know I am alive, they won't stop until they find me. My family would always be in danger.

"The Martelé have yet to appoint their next

leader. The next in the bloodline is too young to take over. Therefore, it goes between three cousins. Their challenge is to find you. Whoever gets your head is the new leader.

"Fuck!" Alex bangs his fist against the wall. "See what you have done, Leo? You had to have that phone!"

Fury builds inside me. "Just leave, Alex. This doesn't concern you. Nobody knows you are still alive. Go back to your wife."

"Doesn't concern me! You are my brother. The whole reason I am here in the first place!"

Alex punches me square in the jaw. I return it with a punch to his stomach. He then charges towards me but is thrown to the floor by Van, who has ripped his restraints from the chair.

"Enough!" Van shouts. "If you continue with this, there will be no need for the Martelé to come after you. You need to work together. Come up with a plan."

Alex charges towards Van, but Van throws one punch to the side of his head, and Alex stumbles, losing his balance.

"Van!" I dive to catch my brother, preventing him from hitting his head on the floor in his unconsciousness.

"He will be fine. He needed taking down a peg or two."

I remove my jacket and place it under Alex's head while he regains consciousness.

Van explains what he has heard in regard to the Martelé knowing I am still alive.

"The new Chief of Police is an old acquaintance of Marco. Marco trusts him. Well, more than the last one anyway. He told Marco the Martelé approached him and offered him money and security if he told them what he knew. Thankfully he doesn't know anything, and Marco already has him in his pocket. His wife works for Mia at the sanctuary. I then did some digging around. There was a leak at air traffic control. The Martelé have had someone tracking the jet. The location was not found, as all evidence was destroyed, but they managed to get hold of one of the air stewards, who admitted she had seen you. She was found dead in her home two days ago."

"The source at air traffic control?"

"No longer breathing."

"Nobody as yet knows our location?"

"No. But like I said, it didn't take me long to find you."

I pace the room again, racking my brain for a solution. Any kind of plan to keep my wife and children safe.

"You need protection, boss," Van admits. "What's the plan?"

"We go back." Alex' grunts as he sits up from his lying position. "It's our only option." He rubs the side of his head where Van knocked him out.

"No. I will not take my family back there to be slaughtered."

"You're just going to wait for them to come here and do it, then?"

"I will protect them."

"How? When an army of Martelé turn up at your house, while your children and wife are sleeping in their beds, how are you going to protect them?"

"I have guns." I'm getting more aggravated by my brother who, unfortunately, is right.

"You have guns." It's Alex's turn to laugh now. "What about when they launch a missile straight through your son's window that blows up the entire house?"

The thought makes me sick to the stomach. What have I done?

"If you come back to the Guerra, we can protect you."

"And how are you going to do that, Van? You and Marco have already destroyed the organisation."

Van looks annoyed at my outburst. He takes a moment and then explains his plans. "We have the new Chief of Police in our pocket. That was a big downfall with the last one who was with the Martelé. We have the government on our side, with new deals happening as we speak. Recruitment has already started. We have pulled in all our men from across the continent and have a new training programme in place. One of which is with Ministry of Defence, who is sending all recent discharged armed forces to us."

The plan sounds commendatory. But I'm surprised at how quickly this has come about and why it hadn't been done before the chaos that unfolded, resulting in me being summoned to Italy.

"I know what you are both thinking," Van continues. "But Marco has his head on straight now. We were attacked from too many sides before, what with the Martelé and Lorenzo, the last Chief of police who corrupted the government. Don't forget the greatness of the Guerra name, which has been created over countless generations. The Guerra isn't just about the size that we are. It's about what we stand for. The country loves us. We do more for the civilians than the Martelé, the police, and the government put together. We have the backing, so we have the power."

"The man talks some sense," Alex agrees.

"It seems you have everything under

control. But I still don't see how my family would be safer there. As soon as we land, the Martelé would target them. They would live a life in fear. You said it yourself. The Martelé don't know where we are. They may never find us."

Van and Alex look at each other.

Alex stands and brushes himself down. "This has been a lot to take in. We need to think about everything before making any decisions. Van, you return to Italy. I will discuss the best route with you. We don't want you being tracked back. When you return, continue with your plans and get them done quickly. We need the Guerra strong. For now, we are safe. But we will come up with a plan for if or when that changes." Alex looks to me for agreement.

I nod.

Alex continues. "Van, you will keep your ears to the ground, and anytime you hear about Leo and his whereabouts, you ring the radio phone. We will set certain times so it will never be missed again. Agreed?" Alex looks to both Van and me.

"Yes."

"Affirmative." Van salutes Alex in a condescending way.

"You were always annoying as a kid, Van. Hey, did you ever learn to ride that bike of yours?"

Van grows red in temper at Alex's remark. The memory of us playing out on our bikes as kids burns brightly in my memory. Van and his sister Mia are the children of my father's number one. When my father was in charge, their mother and my mother spent a lot of time together, so us children were forced to get along. Van was big even as child and could never quite get the art of riding a bike. It was like his wide frame was too large for such a narrow frame.

"No, I broke it after I wrapped it around your head. I then started cage fighting. More of a manly sport than cycling."

Alex still bears the scar across his forehead from when Van threw his bike at him. Alex was a very good cyclist and often teased Van. He competed professionally for a while. Hence Van's reply.

Alex shakes his head. "Right. You get back to your wife and children. Van and I will finish up here. Take the car. I'll sort my own way back."

Alex throws me his car keys, and I catch them with ease.

"Will you two behave?" I ask, hoping Alex doesn't still plan on escorting him off the island and disposing of his body.

"Yes, boss," they both reply in unison.

Katie

"They've been gone a while?" I say to Vanna, more of a question than a statement as I watch her read a message on her phone.

"Yes, Alex said they had to run an errand. But Leo is on his way back now."

"An errand? What kind of errand?"

"I'm not sure, but like I said, Leo is on his way back, so I'm going to leave you to all to rest now." Vanna says goodbye to Mark, not that he's paying any attention, too busy watching cartoons on the television.

"Thank you for coming. Will I see you again soon?"

"Of course. I will pop in tomorrow."

"Great. See you then."

Vanna gives me a hug and leaves.

An unsettled feeling starts in my stomach. Where is Leo? Just as I begin to worry, Leo walks through the door.

"La mia ragazza." *My girl*. Leo's face lights up when he looks at me, and the unsettled feeling disappears.

"Where have you been? We've missed you."

"Papa," Mark shouts and runs over to his father to hug his legs.

Leo picks him up and kisses his head. "I have been preparing for your return home," he tells me. "The doctor said that, providing your test results are fine tomorrow, he will discharge you."

"Thank goodness. I can't wait to get back into a routine. Mark is climbing the walls, being stuck in here."

Leo laughs as Mark climbs his shoulders. "Yes, we need to get this little monkey back to chasing those goats."

"What have you got there?" I ask, noticing a bag in Leo's hands.

"These are for us. Mobile phones. One for you and one for me. Not that I plan on leaving you again, but I would feel better if we had a way of contacting each other at any time."

"Thank you."

And I agree that it's time. Leo was very against us getting phones when we first moved here. Safety, I suppose, as phones are trackable. But he is obviously feeling more secure about having them now. Maybe it has something to do with Alex and Vanna being here.

Leo takes two phones out of the bag and passes one to me. They are unwrapped and switched on. I was expecting a brand-new one in a box.

"Are they second-hand?" I don't mean to sound ungrateful, but it's been a long time since I had a new phone. The excitement of opening a new phone and peeling the screen sticker off is the best feeling.

"Yes, they are new. I've just set it up ready for you. My number, Alex's, and Vanna's are already in your contacts."

"Okay. Thanks." Lighting up the screen, I see it's an iPhone. Thank goodness. I've never been an Android girl. But there aren't many apps. In fact, the only thing on here is the green phone icon to make calls and the messaging speech bubble.

"Where are all the apps?"

Leo dismisses my concern. "No apps. Just calls and text. You don't need anything else."

Mark has gone back to his cartoons, and Leo is now standing over the cot cradling our new baby.

Feeling a little disappointed that I don't get to play *Candy Crush*, I decide to be happy that at least Leo is letting me have a phone. Baby steps.

"Have you had any more thoughts on his name?" I'm really getting sick of everyone calling this baby Smith. A name that isn't even ours.

"How about Zander?"

The name surprises me. It's not one we've discussed or I've heard often. But I like it.

"So instead of Alex, short for Alessandro, Zander short for Alessandro?" I can't help but smile as I ask, this means Leo has made peace with Alex.

"Yes, do you like it? Because if not, we can choose something else."

"No, I love it." I smile.

Leo places little Zander in my arms and then wraps his arm around me. We both stare at our second bundle of love.

"Zander Smith," I say, while really thinking Zander Guerra. Wow. Zander Guerra really does sound like a mafia son. Thank goodness my boys will never live a life so dangerous. "It's perfect, Leo. Ti amo." *I love you.*

"Ti amo." *I love you.*

The next day, all my test results come back fine. I'm pleased to be going home with my little family of four. Leo hasn't let me lift a finger. He changed and dressed the boys and packed all my things. Much to my annoyance, he even dressed me, but you can't argue with Leo Guerra—sorry, Smith.

A nurse pushes me to the exit in a wheelchair. In front of me, Leo walks proudly, carrying a car seat containing Zander while holding Mark's hand. The nurses and patients he passes do a double-take. His muscular, six-foot frame, dark hair, and handsome face demand attention. Smiling to myself, I look at my boys. *My boys*. I'm the luckiest woman in the world.

Once Leo has safely fastened the boys into the car, he lifts me out of the wheelchair and carefully places me in the front seat of our SUV.

"Are you comfortable?" Leo examines my face.

"Yes, thank you."

After double-checking my seat belt and kissing me gently on the lips, he rounds the car and gets in.

"Let's get you home."

It doesn't take long. And the scenery on the way fills me with happiness. It's a coastal drive with beautiful green trees and colourful flowers on one side and clear blue sea and white sand on the other. The windows are open in the car, adding to the sensation. The smell of the sea air and sound of the waves and birds are glorious. What a beautiful place to bring up our children.

Leo parks the car at the front of our house. As I study the door, grateful to be home, I notice something.

"Leo, what's that?" I point to the black-and-white cylinder attached to the porch roof.

Without looking in the direction I am pointing, he replies, "It's just a camera. I've had a couple fixed up around the house. Now that Mark is on the move at lot and with you not being as mobile for a while, I thought it would be helpful to keep an eye on everyone."

A small part of me is a little concerned. Leo has never once been bothered about safety since we arrived. He always said we were safer without technology. But then, maybe it's because he thinks we are so safe, we can use technology again. I'm definitely grateful for a mobile phone. I couldn't cope when I had no contact with Leo. And maybe cameras will be helpful to keep an eye on the boys. Mark does have a tendency to run off.

Leo gets me out of the car first. Leaving Mark strapped in the car is a much safer option than getting him out and letting him run free in the house. I don't think it will be long, however, until he is able to unfasten himself. As if I am going to break, Leo gently lifts me from the car and carries me into the house, heading for the stairs.

"Where are you going?" I ask.

"Taking you to bed. Bed rest for the next two days, apart from when the physios come. Doctor's orders."

"Yes, but bed rest doesn't need to be in an actual bed. Can't we make up a bed on the sofa so I can be with you and the boys?"

Leo stops in his tracks. "It would be easier to look after you all if you're all on the same level.

"Exactly."

Thankfully I was at the hospital when I had my cardiac arrest, so doctors were able to work on me straight away, and it didn't take long for my heart to beat independently again. The doctors are sure I will make a full recovery and not have any long-term health issues, which is amazing, but I just have to take these next few weeks very slowly.

Leo lays me comfortably on the sofa in the living room. From here, I have a good view out of the bifold doors that lead out into the garden and on into the vineyard, and I can also see into the kitchen through the double doors. Perfect. Once the boys are inside, Zander asleep in his crib at my side and Mark playing happily at the kitchen table, Leo covers me with a blanket.

Watching him care for my children and me fills my heart with so much love. To see him now, this loving, doting father and husband, you would never believe he was the boss of the Guerra. That he has tortured and killed many people. Okay, they all deserved it in one way or another, but to look at him now, you would think he wouldn't hurt a fly.

A notification chimes on Leo's phone. "Alex is here." He goes to the front door and lets him in.

"Hi, Katie. I'm not staying. Just thought I would pop in and see if you needed anything?"

"Thanks, Alex. I have no idea. Leo's been taking care of everything. Is there anything we need, Leo?"

"I think we have everything we need."

"Oh, Alex, we've decided on a name. Haven't we, Leo?" I gesture to Leo to introduce Zander.

Leo takes the hint and picks him up. "Uncle Alex, meet your nephew, Zander."

Alex takes Zander and looks at Leo, who nods, confirming he is named after his uncle.

"From the moment I got pregnant, Leo wanted to call him Alex. It had been his choice of name all the way through my pregnancy. But when we found you, we decided Alex may get a little confusing.

"Zander is perfect. I'm honoured. Thank you" His voice breaks a little when he speaks.

Alex and Vanna don't yet have any children. They are a few years older than us. I'm not sure of their situation, and I don't feel it's appropriate to ask. Not unless they were to bring it up, anyway. They are both really good with Mark and Zander, and they seem to really care for children.

While the boys chat in the kitchen, I let myself doze off, feeling very comfortable, safe and relaxed in my beautiful family home.

Chapter Nine

Katie

A few weeks pass, and I'm feeling great. Leo is still trying to wrap me up in cotton wool, although he is tired, and I can tell he is glad of the help around the house and with the boys. While Leo is a wonderful father and husband, I think he has had enough of being the main carer.

There's a knock at the door, Leo opens it, already smiling, he knows who is behind it. "Alex." Leo embraces his brother.

Both of them seem to light up when they are together. There's another level to their happiness when they are in each other's company. It's Friday evening, and Alex and Vanna have come for dinner. It's become a routine that we all really enjoy. Leo especially. It is wonderful to see how close the brothers are once again. It's like they have never been apart.

Leo and Alex go for their usual walk around the vineyard while Vanna and I prepare the dinner.

Tonight, it's a seafood risotto.

Once the table is laid with fresh bread, olives, and salad, Leo dishes out the risotto. "Ladies, this smells amazing. You've spoilt us as usual."

The evening is wonderful. We all share stories from our past. Some sad, some hilarious. We've really bonded over the past weeks. Before we met, I had been worried that being here without family wasn't enough. I had worried about Leo, as he had started to become quite suppressed. But since he has been around Alex, it's like Leo's spark has returned. I do feel like they have some sort of language only they understand. They look at each other in certain way, and the other seems to read exactly what they mean just from a facial expression. They also take these walks together where they talk and can be gone for hours.

"Since you prepared the food, we will do the dishes." Alex nudges Leo to get up from the table.

They both leave with plates in their hands. But as they approach the dishwasher, both of their phones ping with notifications. I glance down at Leo's screen to see it's a notification of activity in the front garden. Both Leo and Alex look in the direction of the table and then back at each other. They throw the dishes in the sink, quickly grab their phones, and exit the room.

"Stay here," Alex commands as he closes the

door behind them both.

"What's going on?" I ask Vanna, shaken by their reaction.

"I'm not sure."

"Well, I'm going to find out." I stand from the table to follow them, but Vanna catches my arm.

"No. We should stay here with the boys." She gestures to Mark sat happily still eating and Zander asleep in this crib beside the table.

Sitting back down, I try and listen for voices. But I don't hear anything. Vanna stands from the table and goes to the kitchen window. She peers outside into the back garden. It's dark outside, so I doubt she will be able to see anything. She then closes the blinds. The next moment, I hear Leo and Alex. They are laughing. The door opens, and they walk in, each carrying a goat in their arms.

"Looks like Upsy and Daisy fancied a night out tonight." Leo laughs.

"How did they get out to the front?" I gasp.

"We'll go put them back and have a look around."

They take them out of the back door into the garden where their enclosure is.

"Aww, they're so funny. Have they ever escaped before?" Vanna asks.

But I'm not finding it funny at all. Theres something they aren't telling me. I can tell. Even Vanna seems like she knows something I don't.

"Why does Alex have our camera alerts on his phone when Leo hasn't even set them up on mine yet?"

Vanna looks a bit taken back by my question. "I have no idea. You'll have to ask Leo that."

Maybe I'm over thinking all this. Or maybe I'm not, but I will get to the bottom of it. Once the goats are safely back in their pen and the hole they chewed in the fence has been covered up, Vanna and Alex say their goodbyes.

"I'm going to take the boys up to bed, and then I think I'll go too. I'm shattered," I say to Leo.

"Okay. Good night," he says, distracted, and it's not his usual response, which annoys me.

I was going to let it lie, but I have now changed my mind. "What was all that about earlier?"

"What do you mean? All what?"

"The way you and Alex looked at each other when the cameras alerted you to activity at the front door. And why has Alex got our cameras set up on his phone when I haven't even got them on mine?"

"La mia ragazza, non preoccuparti." *My girl, do not worry.*

But when has anyone ever stopped worrying because they have been told to *stop worrying*?

"Alex and I went into our old fight mode. We just wanted to make sure everyone was safe, and they were. We thought it might have been a bear or something."

"A bear? Are there bears on this island?"

"Yes, Alex said there are."

I'm not convinced.

"And hand me your phone. I'll download the app and set the cameras up for you now."

"But why did Alex have our camera alert on his phone?"

"Because he was showing me how it all worked."

While I wait for him to set everything up, I take the boys to bed. I know Leo, and I know when he is hiding something from me. I don't feel like it's anything big, though. I know he is only trying to take care of me, so whatever it is he thinks I don't need to know is his way of protecting me and our boys. I trust him, so let it lie. For now, anyway. Once Mark and Zander are settled, I change into my pj's—shorts and a vest top—and return with both baby monitors to Leo downstairs.

"Is it done?" I ask as I flop down next to him on sofa.

"Yes. You're all set. Did the boys go off okay?"

"Yep, sound asleep as soon as their heads hit the pillow."

Leo spends a few minutes showing me around the app.

"This icon here is for the live view. You can scroll down for each camera. There's one on the front and the back door and one at each side. Tap and pinch to widen, zoom in closer, or move the direction, like this." Leo clicks on the back door camera and zooms in to the goats in their pen. "There's also this little clock here where you can go back through and see what has been recorded."

"Ahh, okay. Let me see."

I scroll through the times on the front door notifications until I see the two little billy goats running around our front lawn. Next, two large Italian men storm out of our front door and chase them around the garden. I can't help the giggles that escape me. The goats really torment Leo and Alex, darting off at the last second, running through their legs, coming together, and then splitting off in different directions.

"What is it? What are you laughing at?"

"You… and Alex…." I can hardly speak through laughter.

"Let me see."

When I show him the video, Leo also finds it

amusing.

"Are you laughing at me, Kat-er-een?"

Oh gosh, I love when he calls me that. His Italian accent is thick as my name almost purrs off his tongue. The hairs on the back of my neck stand up, and I'm suddenly aware of a pulse between my legs.

"Yes, I am, Leo *Guerra*. And what are you going to do about it?" I try to sound confident, but my voice catches in my throat as I speak.

Leo's eyebrows rise in a smirk. He knows exactly what he does to me. "What am I going to do about it? I don't like to be made a fool of, Kat-er-een." He cracks his neck from side to side. He does this to release tension. It's been weeks since we have been passionate, and we both have a lot of sexual tension just bursting to get out.

"Well, I think you looked like a fool being outsmarted by a billy goat."

The distance between us is minimal, and I can feel the heat from his body as his arousal grows. He moves his arm along the back of the sofa and grips the back of my neck firmly but gently. He pulls me slightly towards him as he leans in.

His mouth presses against my ear. "La mia ragazza." *My girl.* "Don't tease me. You know I cannot control myself around you. It's too soon. You're not ready." His accent is thick and his voice low with lust.

His words tip me over the edge. Taking hold of his other hand, I guide it onto my leg. He squeezes my thigh as his breathing becomes deeper in my ear. I shuffle my bum down on the sofa, spreading my legs wider, and I move his hand up to my stomach. Lifting the waistband on my shorts, I direct his fingers to the heat in between my legs. He nestles his head into the crook of my neck. He kisses my skin as a groan escapes him. At first his hand doesn't move. But I press my pulsing core towards his hand, and he then slides one of his fingers through my centre.

"Ahh, you're so wet." His teeth graze my neck in his impatience.

"See, I am ready. Ready for you."

I grip his head and forcefully plant my lips on his. Our mouths open hungrily, moans escaping us both. His fingers begin to work their magic, teasing my folds open and swirling my clit. Our kissing reaches another level as our arousal peaks. When I buck into his hand uncontrollably, he gets the message and slides a finger inside me. A gasp escapes my lips as his large finger fills the space that has yearned for him. He goes deep into my heat. I'm hot and wet. But it's not enough. I need more.

Breaking our kiss and removing his hand, I then rise to my knees and push him back into his seat. For a moment the expression on his face is disappointment, but that soon changes when I reach for his shorts, pull down the waistband, and remove his thick length. I wrap my hands around it. It's hot and silky smooth. A bead of excitement releases from the tip, and I instantly wrap my mouth around it, desperate for a taste of what is to come. Leo's hips naturally rise in my direction. As I take him deeper into my mouth, I feel his erection grow larger and harder. I grip the base in both hands, which helps me to accommodate his large size. Sliding up and down, I take him as deep as can, my tongue exploring and taking all it can get. He brings his hands to my head and gathers my long blonde hair, which has fanned around his crotch. He bunches all together in one hand, and, holding it tightly, he tips my head back slightly.

"I need to see your face." His voice is desperate.

Our eyes meet, and I stare into his dark irises as he fills my mouth. The look on his face drives me to work harder. It's an expression he only has when he is this aroused, and it turns me on to the extreme. I'm doing his to him. Me. His wife. Only I get to see this look, a look he only has for me, and that is the most powerful aphrodisiac. My mouth waters, and I can't get enough of him. The appreciative noises coming from him let me know he is close.

But Leo stops me just as he is about to

explode. "Wait." He removes himself from my mouth and sits up slightly, cupping my face. "Do you think we could do this together?"

Nodding in agreement, I instantly stand. He removes my shorts and the vest. In turn, I pull his shorts from his thighs and discard them. He opens his legs and lies back.

"You're in control." He holds his cock upright in anticipation.

I can't help the smile on my face as I look at him. My strong, powerful Italian stallion. All mine. His eyes roam my body, and I can tell he is pleased with what he sees. I have always been happy with my body, but have two children, and you can get a little self-conscious. Not that Leo has ever made me feel that way. It's just my own insecurities. But in this moment, I feel like the most beautiful woman in the world. Straddling him, I press my very wet heat against his cock. Taking it into my hands, I circle my entrance with the tip.

The feeling and the sounds of enjoyment from Leo are almost enough to send me over the edge. Positioning myself, I gently relax my body down towards his groin. He slowly fills me, stretching me to the extreme and making me quiver with anticipation. Leo pulls me in and kisses me with hunger. I return the deepness of the kiss as my hips instinctively rotate. Leo's T-shirt suddenly feels too much of a barrier between us, so I remove it quickly as he lifts his arms in acceptance, and skin to skin, we continue our kiss, devouring each other.

My hips' rotation gets quicker, and I can feel myself become wetter as Leo's cock get thicker and harder inside me. He feels as if he could burst inside me at any moment. The sensation goes beyond sexual pleasure. It's a connection only we share. Simultaneously, our bodies convulse. Holding each other, kissing, looking into each other's eyes, we explode in a world of euphoria. A world where only Leo and I can go. It may only last a minute. But in that moment, our bodies and spirits connect, and we are one.

After holding each other for a while and appreciating our skin-to-skin contact, Leo nibbles my neck while lifting me from his lap and placing me back on the sofa.

"Stay here. Do not move."

"Okay."

I smile as I watch my naked husband check that all the windows and doors are locked, turn the lights off, and grab a bottle of water from the fridge. He then returns and picks me up, one arm under my legs and one under my arms and round my back. I loop my arms around his neck. I love when he carries me like this. After I quickly pick up the baby monitors as we pass the table, Leo carries me out of the kitchen, through the hall, and up the stairs to our bedroom.

While still holding me, he takes the monitors from me and puts them on my bedside table with the water. Then he takes us into our bathroom, turns on the shower, and walks us under the warm water. Here he sets me down on my feet. Tilting my head back, I enjoy the power of the shower jet gently massaging my head. My eyes are closed, but I can feel Leo's eyes on me.

"You are the most beautiful woman in the world, Mrs Guerra."

"Don't you mean Smith?"

Leo doesn't answer, just groans and kisses me primally. My body unintentionally relaxes into his arms.

Once we've washed each other after having another orgasm each, we exit the bathroom dry but still completely naked. I go to my drawer for some clean pj's.

"No, I want nothing between us," Leo instructs as he pulls back the covers and gestures for me to climb in bed beside him.

"I love you," I say as I walk over, my heart feeling incredibly full and grateful. "I love our life. I'm so happy."

"Good." Leo wraps his arms around me and covers us both. "As long as you are happy, so am I."

While drifting off to sleep, I think about what it means to be happy. There have been so many times in my life when I've mistaken happiness for luxury items, extreme holidays, extravagant gifts, or external validation at work. But that's not what being happy is. It's about finding the joy in the little things. Appreciating the now, being present, and spending time with those who you love and who love you.

This right now. In the arms of my husband, where I feel safe and loved. In our home where our two boys lie safely asleep in their beds in the next room—boys who were made with our love. This is happy. People spend too much of their lives wanting what they haven't got, comparing themselves to others. But life isn't about physical items like fast cars or one-off moments of exhilaration over a holiday. It's about feeling content in our everyday life, appreciating the little things. This is what it is to be free, to be happy.

Chapter Ten

Katie

"Hi, Vanna. Just checking if I need to bring towels or anything for the boys?"

"No, we've plenty of towels. I've loads of snacks and food for us and Mark. Just get over here quick so we can have a cocktail."

"Okay, great. I'll be half an hour."

After ending the call to Vanna, I rush about, packing everything but the kitchen sink for Zander. I had forgotten how much stuff a new baby needs. Mark now only has a little backpack with a few snacks and toys in it. We are spending the day at Vanna and Alex's. I say "we," but it's just me and our boys. Leo and Alex are having a lads' day —well, lads' afternoon, so Vanna has invited us to their house. While our house is large and lovely, it's more of family home and cosy. Their house is extreme modern luxury with huge outdoor and indoor swimming pools and floor-to-ceiling windows.

We've popped in a few times but never stayed long. Alex and Vanna usually come to our house, as it's easier with the boys. But today we are spending the day there, and I'm quite excited. Mark is going to love playing in the pool all day, and Zander—well, he can sleep in the shade. Vanna loves helping out, so I'm sure I'll have time to put my feet up in the sun and drink a cocktail or two, seeing as Zander actually prefers a bottle.

The security system alerts us to someone at the door. Alex. Leo lets him in.

"Hi, Alex," I greet him. "Looking forward to your lads' day?"

"Yes, we've lots of fun things planned."

"Oh yeah? What is it you're actually doing? Leo hasn't said."

Alex seems on edge when he answers, like he is hiding something. "Oh, er, you know. Drinking. Watching sports. That kind of thing."

They're definitely not watching *sports*. What man calls them *sports*, anyway? They'd say football or rugby. They're probably going shooting or something they think I won't agree with. But I trust Leo, so I don't let it bother me.

Leo helps me load the car with the boys' bags. We then get them both strapped into their car seats. Leo checks and double-checks that their belts are firmly fastened and the seats securely fitted into the car.

"We are going now. Make sure you take your phone. I've got mine. I'll check in with you later. Take care. Ti amo." *I love you.*

He gives me a kiss and then gets in Alex's car. Alex beeps his horn as he drives away. I wave them off, cursing, as the noise has woken Zander, and he is now screaming in the back seat. But as soon as I start the engine and set off, the movement of the car settles him back down. Mark and I sing nursery rhymes on the short journey to Vanna's. Mark is very excited to see Vanna and play in her pool.

Vanna is waiting for us when we pull up to their house. She comes straight to the car and opens Marks door.

"Va Va!" Mark screams excitedly, pulling at his seat belt to get to her.

"Hello, handsome. I've been waiting for you." Vanna unclips him and helps him out of the car.

Vanna and Alex's home is like a show home. Its pristine grey marble floors and white walls are almost clinical, which has me worrying about Mark's sticky fingers. There is a grand, open entrance hall which is flooded with light from the floor-to-ceiling windows and a staircase that looks to be floating in mid-air.

Vanna leads us through to the back of the

house and into the large, white ultra-modern dining kitchen. Huge bifold doors open out onto a pristine patio with tiles the same as those inside leading to the garden and infinity swimming pool. The house is higher up on the island than ours. We wanted to be able to walk straight from our garden and be on the beach. But here the views are spectacular. You can't tell where the swimming pool ends and the sea begins.

"Wow, Vanna, your home is beautiful." I have been a couple of times before, but only to pop in, and I've always had my eyes on Mark. I knew it was lovely, but this is spectacular.

"Thank you, but it's more the view that makes it special. Come, I've set up an area by the shallow end of the pool in the shade."

"Perfect."

While I get Zander settled in his pram, Mark pulls out of Vanna's hand in excitement. He jumps straight into the pool. Luckily I know my son well and fastened his life jacket onto him before we got in the car.

"He's no fear at all. Worries me to death, he does." I sigh.

"Well, he's got Guerra blood." Vanna laughs.

"So, how long have you lived here?"

"Since we arrived, actually. We bought the land from the farm next door, just over that hill.

There was only a small rundown cottage here then. We lived in that while we built this and then knocked it down to build the swimming pool."

"Gosh, did you design it all yourself?"

"Yes—well, between me and Alex. We had a lot of time on our hands, so we did the majority of the work ourselves as well."

"And now you own a gym?"

"Yes, Alex and I run the fitness centre. We needed something to do, and we are both into fitness. We mostly do strength training and self-defence classes. It seems to be very popular on the island."

"Yeah, I'm sure."

"Right, cocktails. What do you like?"

"Anything, really, but nothing too sweet and not strong. I've not had a drink since I got pregnant with Zander, and I need to drive home."

"Okay, I'll see what I can do."

While Vanna crushes ice and squeezes lemons at the bar beside the pool, I give Mark his pool toys and splash about with him for a few minutes. He absolutely loves water. He can pretty much swim now, but I'd never let him in water without a vest just yet.

"Here we are. One lemon drop cocktail specially made by me."

"Oooh, lemon drop. I don't think I have had one of those before. What's in it?"

"Just try it."

As I take a sip, my taste buds are met with a delightful blend of sweet and tart.

"It's good," I say as I take another sip, enjoying the sharp, refreshing taste of lemon balanced beautifully with the sugar around the glass.

"I knew you would like it. Vodka, Cointreau, fresh lemon juice, simple syrup, sugar on the rim, and a lemon wedge for garnish. But I didn't put as much of the alcohol in yours, so I topped it up with a splash of soda water."

"Thank you, it's perfect."

"It was my mother's favourite drink. Although the lemons in Italy are much better than we can get here."

"Yeah, that is true about Italy. We've be growing our own lemons, and Leo's been doing everything exactly as he did back there, but they're just not the same. He can't get them to grow as big or be as sweet."

Flashbacks of lemons in Italy fill my mind. When Leo actually asked me to marry him, we were surrounded by his lemon trees. He'd undressed me and laid me on the ground beneath them. Then he'd pulled a lemon from the tree and sliced it open with a knife. He'd squeezed it intensely, so the juice ran down his arm and on to my naked body. He'd then proceeded to lick my body clean.

"Earth to Katie. Hello?" Vanna pulls me out of my memory just in time.

"Oh, sorry. I was miles away."

"In Italy?"

"Yes, Italy."

"I miss it too." Vanna sighs.

"Really? But you've got the perfect life here."

"We've got the perfect house with the perfect view. We've got jobs we enjoy and have enough money to have whatever we want. But those are things, not life."

"No, I suppose not."

"I love Alex, but I miss having family around me. Well, some of them. I miss having friends. What's the point in having this big house if we have no one to share it with?"

"I understand what you mean. But you have us now." I raise my glass in a toast to Vanna.

She accepts, and we clink glasses.

She's smiling, but there's sadness behind it. "Anyone on the outside looking in would think this is the perfect life. But it's like *Groundhog Day* or like going on holiday and staying there for the rest of your life. It's repetitive and boring. I have nothing to look forward to. Every day is the same. Nothing will ever change. Until I get old and can no longer do the things I can now."

Vanna speaks with real sadness. I'm taken aback and not really sure what to say.

"I wanted children," she continues. "I wanted a family. But that has all been taken away from me."

"What do you mean?"

"We've been trying for years. Nothing. We went to all the doctors we could, we've had test after test. Turns out, my reproductive organs are older than their years, and Alex has a low sperm count."

"But there are things that you can do to help that, right?" I ask hopefully, but Vanna shakes her head.

"We've done all the fertility treatments the island has to offer. Medications, injections, supplements. Nothing worked. What we need is IVF, but the hospital on the island doesn't have the facilities or specialist for that."

"Oh, Vanna, I'm so sorry."

"Thanks, but please don't tell me it will happen eventually or to stop trying and it will happen, etc. I've had enough of that from councillors and random people, and it really doesn't help."

"No, of course."

Vanna puts on her sunglasses and takes a big sip of her cocktail. I expect she's covering the emotion in her eyes.

"Don't give up hope, though, Vanna. Miracles do happen. I'm a firm believer in everything happening for a reason."

"Yeah, we will see." Vanna slumps back in her chair.

Leo

As soon as Alex pulls the car away from our house, I go into work mode. "The latest updates in Italy?" I ask.

"As of this morning, we have restored all connections and gained new trade deals. Van has the new recruits in training, and there has been a restructure in ranks. The Guerra is going to be bigger and stronger than ever."

"Any more developments on the fact that I am still alive?"

"Nothing," Alex assures me. "Van has ears everywhere. But that's not necessarily a good thing. And without telling people exactly what they are listening for, it's hard to dig for more information."

"Still, it buys us some time."

"No, it doesn't." Alex groans, shaking his head. "There are new people arriving on the island every week. There's only so much background we can check. They turn up with fake passports and new identities, just like you and me. We can keep an eye on unplanned arrivals, but those arranged through correct channels, we have no control over. Martelé could have people arriving any day now, and we wouldn't have a clue."

Alex pulls off the main road and up a dirt track. The road has a steep incline. The higher we go, the more incredible the views of the island get. It's a mixture of greens from the luscious trees and plants and blues from the sky and ocean. I take in the sight as my brain processes Alex words.

We need to return to Italy soon. The Martelé must not find us here. They cannot ever know this island exists. My Katie is not going to be happy when I tell her. She is going to be devastated, in fact. Our life on this island is all she has ever wanted. All she has ever wanted for our boys. And I am about to take all that away from her. I'm furious with myself that I have brought about this situation. The reason they are in danger is that I returned to Italy. I wasn't careful enough. I was seen. My return even resulted in the death of an innocent air stewardess. My head hangs in shame, and I rub my forehead.

"Hey, you can cut that out." Alex elbows me in the side. "We are Guerras. We don't worry or care about situations. We get things done and move on."

"How do you know what I am thinking?"

"I can see guilt all over your face. Snap out of it. Where are your Guerra balls? You better put that shit to bed before we leave this island, or you will get us all fucking killed."

He stops the car. We've reached the top of a small mountain. It's a shooting range. Alex gets out of the car and greets a tall, thin man in a very worn camouflage outfit. While they greet each other, I get out and have a look around.

There are three outdoor shooting ranges, each with various shooting distances. There's a large metal barn that appears to house an indoor shooting range, and there is also a thick, steel shipping container that, I imagine, stores the weapons and ammunition.

Alex finishes his conversation and joins me, slapping me on the back as he approaches. "Let's see what you got, then, little brother."

As I expected, the shipping container contains a variety of guns and ammunition.

"Get yourself a rifle, a pistol, and a shotgun," Alex instructs as he picks up a shotgun and manoeuvres it around in his hands.

After a few minutes, I have selected some equipment I like the look of. The thin man who goes by the name of Hank sets us up in one of the bays. The targets, silhouettes of heads and shoulders, are several hundred feet away.

Hank runs though some safety precautions, but I don't listen. I can't hear him for the adrenaline that rushes through my body while I'm holding the rifle.

I've always had my gun with me at home, and I would often get it out of my safe and hold it, but it has been years since I fired a gun. Years since I inflicted gruelling pain or even death. The excitement of what's to come has my heart beating so hard, I can hear it in my ears.

I bring the rifle up to my shoulder. I grip firmly with my right hand and support its weight with my left. Aligning my eyes with the target, I wrap my index finger around the trigger and fire.

One. Two. Three.

The sound, the adrenaline. The powerful equipment in my arms brings back feelings I hadn't realised I'd missed. It feels good. It feels natural.

Alexs laughs as he sees the two eyes and the nose I have created in my target. "Not bad, Leo. Not bad at all."

"It's like riding a bike," I say.

"Well, let's hope Van doesn't shoot as well as he rides a bike."

"He's a loyal man, Van is," I reply protectively.

"I know, I know. I'm just having a joke."

"Let's see what you're made of, then."

Alex also fires his rifle three times—one straight in the middle of the forehead, one in the centre of the chest, and one in the groin area.

"Not bad," I comment sarcastically.

It seems neither of us have lost our touch. We spend the next few hours, trying out different guns and shooting them from various ranges. I leave feeling exhilarated.

"You enjoyed that, didn't you?" Alex asks as we start the journey down the mountain.

"I did."

"It's in our blood. We belong in Italy. We are the Guerra."

"You're glad to go back, aren't you?"

"I never wanted to leave. I did it for you and Vanna," he admits.

"It might be in my blood, but it isn't a life I would have chosen. It's not a life I would choose for my children."

"Your boys can choose their own path. We aren't like Papa. We would never force our children to become something they are not or willingly put them in danger. There're ways of protecting Mark and Zander. We will keep them at a safe distance." Alex turns and looks at me. "Just because we are returning to Italy doesn't mean your life has to change. Yes, there will be a lot to deal with on our return. But once things settle down, I will take my position as leader, and you can take on as much or as little responsibility as you wish."

"You will take over as leader?" Although I don't want to return to the role of the don, I'm annoyed at Alex's presumption that he will return and take the lead. After all, he has never been the boss of the Guerra. He was next in line before me, but when he died, he left that responsibility on me.

"Yes. It is my duty. I am the eldest in the Guerra."

"And what about Marco, the current leader?"

"He will step aside for the true heir. After all, he hasn't exactly been doing a sufficient job."

I crack my neck at Alex's words. Not only do I have the Martelé to deal with on our return, but I also have my big brother. I had forgotten how arrogant he can be. Deciding not to argue at his point, I ask, "When do you suggest we leave?"

"As soon as possible. We need our return to be as big a surprise to the Martelé as possible."

"Oh, I think they will be surprised, especially when they find out Vanna is alive. How exactly are you going to play that one?"

"She is going to take over the Martelé, of course."

Nothing leaves my mouth as I stare at Alex in disbelief. Does he really think the Martelé are going to allow Vanna walk back in there and hand over the lead to her? He has lost his head.

"You're out of your mind." I shake my head as I exit his car which, is now parked in his driveway.

Alex laughs. "You'll see. Italy is ours, brother."

"When are you going to tell Katie?" Alex asks as we enter his home.

"Tell me what?" My wife's voice appears out of nowhere, followed by her long, tanned legs, which make their way down the stairs in front of me. She has Mark in one hand, wearing his pyjamas, and his bag in the other. She has obviously just gotten him changed.

"Nothing to worry about at the moment, la mia ragazza." *My girl.* I give her kiss on the lips. She tastes of her usual sweetness mixed with a little lemon. She tastes like home.

"Hmm," Katie murmurs, raising her eyebrows at my dismissive answer.

Katie

I thought there was something, but I couldn't put my finger on it. Now I know for definite that Leo is hiding something from me, and Alex knows about it. I wonder if Vanna knows what it is too. I hate secrets. I hate not knowing things. But given we're at Vanna and Alex's house, now isn't the time to discuss it.

Vanna and I have had a lovely afternoon. Mark has really enjoyed playing in the swimming pool. Vanna and I took it in turns to play with him in the water, throwing him about and having races. Mark is very tired from all the excitement, and now that he's dried and in his nightwear, I have no doubt he will be asleep soon. We all walk through the house and out into the pool area. Vanna is sat in the shade, giving Zander his bottle.

"Look who I found," I say to Vanna, gesturing to Alex and Leo behind me.

"You're back. Did you have fun?" she asks.

"What exactly have you been doing?"

But neither of them directly answers my question.

"Bonding, and we thoroughly enjoyed ourselves," Alex says, putting an arm around Leo's shoulder. He then gets cigars out of his jacket pocket and hands one to Leo.

My eyes bore into the side of Leo's head, but he purposely doesn't give me eye contact, knowing full well I will disapprove. That doesn't stop him from taking the lighter Alex offers and igniting the cigar in his mouth. A cloud of smoke surrounds him, and suddenly I'm transported back to a time in Italy when Leo was different to the man I married.

"So, Katie. You still haven't told me how you and Leo got together," Vanna remarks from where she sits, happily winding Zander on her knee.

But I can't take my eyes off Leo. Something has changed in him. He and Alex talk quietly to each other and make their way over to the outside bar, out of eyesight .

"Oh, you know, the usual mafia love story. He kidnapped me, kept me prisoner, took away my passport so I couldn't leave, and forced me to marry him."

Vanna laughs at my reply but stops uncomfortably when she looks behind me. A glass smashes on the floor, but I don't turn to look. No doubt Leo has heard my answer, and from the look on Vanna's face, he is not amused.

"I think it's time we were going," Leo's voice booms from behind me.

"But we've not eaten yet." Vanna stands hopefully.

"The boys are tired. We need to get them to bed." Leo gathers up their things and puts it all in their bags.

"Thank you for having us, Vanna. But like Leo said, the boys have had a lovely but busy day, so I think we better get them home." Not speaking to Leo, I also gather more of their things and put Zander in the pram.

"I'll take the pram and get them into the car." Leo says, then disappears into the house with the boys and Alex, leaving me with Vanna.

She looks at me sympathetically. "Is everything okay?"

"I think you know as well as I do, Vanna, that something is going on, and until I know what it is, everything is not okay."

Vanna nods and gives me a hug. "Everything will be just fine. You'll see."

But her words worry me even more.

After saying goodbye, we leave. We don't say a word to each other on the way home or after we go into the house. We just fall into the routine of getting the boys settled for bed, making their milk, reading them a bedtime story, then a trip to the bathroom for Mark and a change for Zander.

It's not until they are both asleep and we

go downstairs that I finally look at Leo. His face is angry. He stands tall in the kitchen and looks down at me wide-eyed.

"What was that?" he demands.

"What was what?"

Leo bangs his fists on the kitchen worktop. "You know very well. Disrespecting me in front of Vanna and my brother."

"It's hardly disrespect when it is the truth, Leo." I'm mad. I'm furious at the way he is speaking to me. How dare he. "What is going on with you?" Emotion fills my voice now, and I see a flash of regret in his eyes.

His shoulders relax slightly, and he takes a seat at the island. "Sit down, Kat-er-een." He pulls out the stool beside him. "I am sorry."

His words hit me in the gut. I'm not going to like what comes next.

"My actions have put you and our boys in danger."

He isn't looking at me when he speaks, so I take hold of his hand because although his words scare me, I trust him. "What has happened? Tell me everything. Don't leave anything out. I need to understand."

Leo begins by explaining the turmoil the Guerra has been through. He tells me about Mia's disappearance and Marco falling apart. Listening intently, I don't speak, just give his hand a little squeeze every now and then to encourage him to continue, which he does.

"When you weren't answering the phone, I didn't think rationally. I needed to get back to you immediately. I didn't cover my tracks. I may have led the Martelé right to us." Leo hangs his head in shame.

My heart is racing, and my mind is in overdrive at the thought of our babies in danger. "Okay. What now, then, Leo Guerra?" I ask firmly and expectantly.

Leo's eyes instantly meet mine, searching for my anger and annoyance, which is there, but I'm hiding it. Honestly, when my boys are safe, I will let my anger out at Leo for going back to Italy in the first place. But for now, I need him to think logically, to protect our children.

"We go back to Italy."

Chapter Eleven

Leo

We take five boat journeys to different islands within the Caribbean Sea and Atlantic Ocean to ensure Nuova Vita Island's location is kept a secret. We then board a private plane in Jamaica that takes us to Cuba. The journey so far has taken twenty-four hours, so we lay low in a villa in an emerald forest. It's a hidden paradise home to lush greenery, so the only thing that will see us here is the wildlife.

While Katie settles the boys into their beds, I watch her intently. She's hardly spoken to me since yesterday when I told her that we needed to go back to Italy. Once I explained that returning was our only option to ensure our safety, she insisted on leaving straight away. I'm still waiting for her to lose her temper or get upset. Her reaction wasn't what I expected. She's so calm. Too calm. I worry about her health, her heart. It wasn't long ago that I nearly lost her. My chest pounds with guilt.

The sound of my phone ringing distracts me

from my wife. When I take the device out of my pocket, I see Alex's name lighting the screen.

"Sshh!" Katie waves me out of the room, the noise disturbing Mark.

I go out onto the balcony and close the door quietly before I answer. "Alex."

"Have you arrived?"

"Yes. Katie's is settling the boys in bed."

"Good. You two get to bed as well. You need to be up and out early, as the jet is scheduled to leave Cuba at 8:00 a.m."

This I already know because I arranged it. I'm getting tired of my brother's orders. After Katie deciding last night that we needed to leave immediately, I phoned Alex, who came straight round and helped me organise our return journey while Katie packed the necessities. We decided it would be better if Katie, the boys, and I travelled separately to Alex and Vanna. Alex said he needed to sort some things out along with finding homes for our animals before they left, so the two of them are leaving tonight via a different route than us.

"We are leaving the house now. I'll check in with you again tomorrow."

I end the call and place my phone back in my pocket. I have the urge to light a cigar. But I know it will infuriate Katie if I go back in smelling of smoke, so I push my craving aside. Up until

Van called weeks ago, I hadn't had a smoke since moving to the island. That's what stress does to you, I suppose.

The jet is the final leg of our journey. It is taking us back to Italy. The flight is just over eleven hours. Which means it will be 1:00 a.m. the following day when we arrive in Italy. It will be dark and late, which means we should be able to get to the Guerra house without too much trouble. But it won't take long after that for word to get around, that we have in fact returned from the dead.

Taking in the view from the balcony, I appreciate the calm sounds coming from the wind lightly brushing the trees and the birds calling as they return to their nests in anticipation for nightfall. The sun is setting, and the sky is a beautiful shade of pink. The calm before the storm.

When I return to the bedroom, Katie is in bed. She's pretending to be asleep. No doubt to avoid talking to me. I undress and slide in bed next to her. I don't imagine I'll get much sleep, but I'll try.

I am right. No sleep is to be had by either myself or Katie. Our boys have other ideas. What with Zander waking almost every hour for a feed and Mark being disturbed, which then makes him realise we are in an unfamiliar place, we pretty much spend most of the night watching *In the Night Garden* and pacing up and down the bedroom. Ahh, the life of a mafia boss.

Katie

I'm tired. Exhausted, actually, and I feel sick with nerves. Not that you could tell from the outside. I hope not, anyway. I'm trying my hardest to keep it together for my boys. I told Mark that we're going on an exciting holiday. And Zander, well—I'm sure he can sense something, as he doesn't want to be anywhere other than my chest.

We are on the jet for at least the next eleven hours. The jet that seems to have had another makeover since I was last on it. It was always luxurious, but it's even more extravagant now. We enter into the suite area, which is where you need to be for take-off and landing. Well, where you should be for safety reasons. This is where the seats are with seat belts. There are ten chairs in total. Each chair is next to a window. And when I say chair, I don't mean the thin, body-width-sized seat you get in economy flights. I mean cream leather wingback armchairs that spin and recline so far back, they turn into beds. Each of them also has a table that, as if by magic, appears out of the wall so you can use it as a desk or to eat off.

Mark is in his element, pressing all the buttons on the arm of one of the chairs and making a television screen pop up and down from the armrest. I'm hoping after all the excitement, he will settle down for a nap so I can also get my head down for a few hours. Once he's had a tour of the bedrooms, the bathroom, and office space, we all get strapped in for take-off. Mark sits opposite me, and I have Zander on my knee. I give him a bottle so that the sucking helps his little ears not to pop with the pressure.

Leo sits to our right. I can see him staring at me through the corner of my eye. I still haven't said a word to him other than discussing the boys' needs. He's told me the plan for the next forty-eight hours, so that's all I need to know for now. Once we are in the air, Mark's tiredness soon catches up with him. My eyes close as soon as I see him settle. I feel Leo take Zander from my arms, which I appreciate, but I don't say a word, just switch my chair to recline and go to sleep. Five hours pass in an instant, and I'm woken by my stomach rumbling at the smell of mouth-watering food. Garlic and Italian deliciousness fill my nostrils.

"Pizza!" Marks screams in excitement when a beautiful air stewardess parks a very large cart of food beside us.

Jealousy runs through me when I see her eye up Leo and offer him food first.

"No. Ladies and children first," he barks. And I'm soon put at ease when I see his eyes are only for us.

Our tables are laid with an assortment of pizza, pasta dishes, risotto, and salads. Mark is in his element, having a bit of this and a bit of that. He speaks to himself happily. I catch Leo smiling at him proudly.

The rest of the journey is filled with playing hide-and seek-and colouring. Watching Leo being the doting father makes me a little bit sad. I hope our return to Italy doesn't take him away from his boys, I hope he doesn't change. Who am I kidding? Of course he will change. He's the head of the mafia. Or is he? That's a conversation I haven't had with Leo. Will he return and take back the place he left? Will Marco just step aside after all this time? Or will Alex want to take the lead, seeing as he is the eldest brother and would naturally have been leader if he hadn't disappeared? I suppose I will just have to wait and see.

With less than an hour before we land, I decide to take a shower and freshen up.

"I've arranged for some clothes to be put in the master bedroom. There should be everything you need," Leo says as I excuse myself from the madness of toys and laughter.

When you're in the master bedroom, you'd forget you were even on a plane. There's a fake window which is a screen lit up with a picturesque view of the mountains. There is also a king-size bed and a wardrobe where I find a range of designer outfits, all new with tags in my size. It's been years since I wore anything this fancy. My usual attire at home on the island was shorts and a vest top or a floaty sundress, all of which I got from the market or a local dressmaker. But I'm not ashamed to admit I'm a little excited by the luxury items in front of me.

Selecting a fitted red Givenchy dress and black Louboutins, I place them on the bed and then get in the shower. I wash and dry my hair into loose curls and put on a full face of makeup. When I'm dressed, I look at my reflection. I look good, hot, and just like a mafia woman should. The natural, comfy mumsy look is nowhere to be seen. A flutter of nerves builds in my stomach. Taking a deep breath, I lift my head up high and confidently strut back into the suite to find my family.

When I enter, I'm met with the eyes of my husband. He stands from his chair. His eyes roam my body, and I'm sure I hear a growl from within him. His eyes look carnivorous, like he could devour me in any second.

"Get back in that bedroom." Forcefully, he walks me backwards and closes the door behind him.

"Leo, what are you doing? We can't leave the

boys in there alone."

Leo puts his face into my neck and inhales deeply. "I need to have you now."

He rolls his hips into me, and warmth instantly pools between my legs, but I push him away. Not only am I still mad with him, but it's taken me ages to get ready. I'm not having him mess up my hair now. Plus, Mark's in the other room alone, doing goodness knows what.

"No. Get changed. We are landing soon." And I walk out of the room feeling pleased with myself, but also a little needy.

Leo sits down in the chair beside us just as the pilot announces the need to put our seat belts on. He's in his tailored black suit and crisp white shirt and tie. His hair is styled to perfection, he is clean-shaven, and his scent meets my nostrils and instantly makes me quiver. I may be mad with him, but he still turns me on.

When the aircraft comes to stop, I gather our things to get them ready to be collected and make sure our boys are wrapped up for the cool night air.

When the plane door opens, two tall, large men enter. Marco and Van.

I can't help but dash to Marco and put my arms around him. "Just Marco." I squeeze him tightly, and he returns the gesture. "I've missed you," I say, letting him go and enjoying the softness and emotion on his face that took me a long time to earn.

Marco will always have a special place in my heart. He saved my life by risking his, and I will never forget that. Without him being willing to give up his own life for mine, I would not be here.

Feeling Mark at my legs, I pick him up and introduce them. "Mark, this is Marco."

"Hi, Marco. That's like my name but with an Ooo."

"Yes, it is. This is who you are named after. He is a very special friend of ours."

"It's very nice to meet you, Mark."

Marco holds out his hand to Mark, and he takes it. Emotion flutters in my chest at the sight.

"Me, too, Marco. I'm just Mark," he replies.

Both myself and Marco laugh at Mark's innocent yet perfectly hilarious "Just Mark," a nickname I gave Marco all those years ago when we first met.

Leo joins us and shakes Marco's hand. "How're the legs?" he asks.

Marco brushes off Leo's concern. "Good as new."

"Mrs Guerra," Van greets me with a nod before breaking eye contact.

The Guerra's foundation is built on a code of honour, loyalty being the main law or commandment. No one should ever look at the woman of another Guerra, especially one of such a high level. I feel Van is being a little extreme, seeing as we do know each other, but the whole situation is very unusual for all of us. I expect Van is apprehensive about his current position in the hierarchy now that Leo has returned.

"Ready, boss?" Marco asks Leo.

He nods. "Here, put these on." Leo hands me my sunglasses.

I look at him in question. It's gone 1:00 a.m., and it's pitch-black outside.

"No eye contact, no emotion. Remember who you are, Mrs Guerra."

Marco directs us to the door of the plane. "Van will exit first. Then you, then Katie. I will follow behind. Stay close. The car is a few steps away from the end of the stairs. Your pathway is lined with guards. Let's go."

Leo holds Zander, and I hold Mark's hand and take a deep breath. Here we go. I can do this. My heels clink loudly on the metal stairs that take us from the jet to the tarmac, or apron, as it's officially called. Six guards, three on either side, line our way to a black SUV. Each guard stands with a gun in his hand, a sight I don't think I will ever get used to or feel comfortable around. The guards look alert but do not look at us, apart from one, whose eyes I can feel following us. I don't look directly at him, but I can see him in the corner of my eye.

Once my boys are safely fastened in the seats in the car, I breathe a sigh of relief. It's one thing being married to a Guerra, but having children who are Guerra is on another level of worry.

"Does everyone know now that we are alive?" I ask Marco, feeling uneasy about the guard who watched our every move.

"Well, they probably do now. It's been on a need-to-know basis. Everyone knew something was happening, and I'm sure some guessed."

Yeah, the guard was probably just shocked to see us.

It's not long before we are through the manned security gates of the Guerra house and driving down the familiar pebbled driveway. Lights on either side lead us to the house. It's a beautiful building even in the dark. I have some very happy memories of being here. But would I say I'm glad to be back? I'm not sure.

One thing I am looking forward to is seeing my parents. The thought of seeing them fills me with emotion. I feel a stab in the heart over what I must have put them through, but I put it to the back of my mind for now. I need to focus on getting in the house and the boys settled.

Alga and Sergio are waiting at the door to greet us. They each wear big, beaming smiles.

"Mrs Guerra." Alga puts her hands out for a second, but then retracts them, unsure.

But I wrap my arms around her and give her a big squeeze. "It's so good to see you. And you, too, Sergio." I wrap an arm around him, as well, and pull us all together. We have a giggle for a moment, our eyes filled with emotion.

"Katie," Leo shouts from car.

"Oh, the boys."

Alga and Sergio follow me to the car and make a fuss over Mark and Zander.

The house is as beautiful as always. I'm still as much in awe as the first time I saw it. The hallway is bright and airy. It smells floral and a little of paint. They must have spruced it up for our arrival. The marble floors shine impeccably, and the vases burst with colourful floral bouquets.

"I've made the two back bedrooms up for you and the boys. I hope that's all right? They're adjoining rooms, so I thought would prefer that," Alga says as she rocks little Zander in her arms. "Come on, I'll show you. Sergio, bring up the children's bags," Alga instructs her husband. "We only found out you were coming this morning, so it's been a terrible rush. But whatever we haven't got, we can get tomorrow."

Alga opens the door to one of the bedrooms, and it's been painted a lovely shade of turquoise blue. There's a single bed on one side of the room and a cot on the other. There's a changing table and a rocking chair in one corner and a little table and chair in another. Then there are piles of new toys. The carpet looks brand-new as well, and there are little rugs dotted about with trains and cars on them. It's a little boy's paradise.

"Wow, Mummy, look at this. Is this for me?" Mark runs around the room, taking everything in.

"It's perfect, Alga, Sergio. Thank you."

"Mummy, what is that?" Mark stands at the floor-to-ceil window and points outside.

Walking over, I know exactly what he is pointing at. "That, Mark, is a swimming pool."

"We have a swimming pool?" Marks eyes are wider than I've ever seen them. His mouth is wide open, too, as he jumps up and down with joy, making a squeaking sound.

"If you're a good boy tonight and go straight to sleep, you can go for a swim tomorrow."

"Oh yes!" He runs around, punching the air.

I think Mark is going to be happy here.

"Why don't I get the boys ready for bed?" Alga offers. "I've run them a bath, and I'll read them a story. I'm sure you have lots of things to be doing."

Alga is already opening a wardrobe full of brand-new clothes. She selects the boys some pyjamas. Seeing as Mark has only just met Alga and he isn't used to being with anyone other than me and Leo, he has really taken to her, but she does give off a very motherly, kind aura.

"Well, if you don't mind."

"Not at all. I'd love to. And here." Alga passes me a monitor. "It's video, so you can see exactly what they are doing in here and their bathroom. And if you need to speak, you just press this button here."

"Thank you."

They have thought of everything. Feeling happy my boys are in good hands, I go downstairs in search of Leo. I find him in his office with Marco and Van.

Leo

"Alex will arrive tomorrow afternoon. Gather everyone at the west shore warehouse in the morning. All Guerra men must be there, apart from a couple of guards who will stay at the house with Katie and the boys. Van, do you think you can manage to explain the situation?"

"Yes, boss."

Katie enters as I speak. I see that Marco and Van expect me to end the conversation with her arrival. But I don't. I continue, "Immediately after, we will have a meeting with the Martelé. We do not want them to be prepared for their ultimatum, so it is imperative that the meeting is right after and they do not find out about Alex and Vanna's return until then."

"What is their ultimatum?" Van asks, but I ignore him.

"Get it done now, Van. Let me know when it is arranged."

Van nods but doesn't leave the room.

"Fucking now, Van."

"Oh right, yes." He shuffles out.

How Marco has tolerated him as his right-hand man for all this time, I do not know.

Marco frowns, and I can tell he has something on his mind.

"What is it? Just spit it out, Marco."

"What is the ultimatum?"

"We get the Martelé to call a truce."

"And if they don't agree?"

"We take them over."

"How?"

"With Vanna. Alex has it all worked out. He

will explain it thoroughly tomorrow."

Then Marco surprises me. "And what if I don't agree?"

I crack my neck and look at him. Reading his expression, I can see he isn't happy. He has his almost-ready-to-explode face on.

"Then we have a problem. Do we have a problem, Marco?"

"No, boss," Marco says, then leaves the room and closes the door a bit harder than needed.

Katie states the obvious. "He's not happy."

"No, he's not."

"So, let me get this straight." Katie walks around my desk and perches on the edge with one leg crossed over the other. "You are going to ask the Martelé to call off the war. And if they say no, you are going to take their territories?"

"It's a bit more complex than that."

"Why would the Martelé give you what you want?"

"Because we have Vanna. Vanna is their true bloodline leader."

"Vanna is a woman. Vanna is supposed to be dead. Do you really think the Martelé will actually care that she is alive?"

"The Martelé may be a disgrace, but they do have values where family is concerned. Vanna has her father's last will and testament. I haven't seen it, but Alex says its foolproof."

"Alex says? Look, Leo, I know he is your brother, but you haven't seen him for many years. You don't really know him. He hasn't ever been a leader, but you have." Katie stands and puts her hands on my forearms and looks up at me. "I'm not happy about being here, but if we have to be, then you need to take control. Don't keep things from Marco. He has always had your back. He has been running the Guerra for years. You need him. He needs you. You need to work as a team. Do not let Alex come in here tomorrow and start bossing you all about. Get it sorted before you go to your meetings. You can't resolve this with the Martelé unless you are one unit."

Katie talks sense. I can't help but smile at my wife. She may not be happy about being here, but she definitely belongs in the Guerra.

"Mrs Guerra. You have never looked sexier." My voice is low with arousal. Gently stoking her arms, I watch her body react to my words and my touch. Her body is completely under my control, and I love it.

"Leo, I'm serious."

She tries to push me away, but I lean my body against hers, pinning her to the desk. "Please do not worry. I have everything in hand."

My mouth goes to hers, and she fights me

for a moment, but her body soon gives in and melts into my arms. While we devour each other's mouths, I pick her up carry her to the door. After locking it, I take her to the chesterfield sofa in the corner of the room.

"That dress has been teasing me ever since you put it on. I don't like to be teased, la mia ragazza." *My girl.* "Remove it."

A smirk appears at the side of my wife's mouth. "No." The refusal is her submission. I like it when we play this game.

"Tssk. Kat-er-een. You know I do not tolerate disobedience." I straddle her, gripping her jaw and kissing her forcefully while I remove the tie from round my neck. Taking both of her hands, I raise them above her head. "You will be punished for your crime. Do you have any final words?" I ask while wrapping my tie around her wrists and hooking them around my neck.

"No," she says again in gasp.

Her anticipation of what is to come has her heat racing and eyes wide. The sight of her arousal is enough to make me blow. Her mouth meets mine hungrily. I enjoy her for a few moments until I pull away. Standing, I lift her and lay her over the side of the office sofa. I lift up her dress to reveal her perfect round ass. I rip her thong off with ease, but she jumps a little in surprise.

"Stay down," I command.

I slap her right ass cheek. Her scream turns to a moan when I massage the area. I treat the other side to the same—pain followed by pleasure. I grip her hips as I push my groin into her crack. I'm still fully clothed, and I'm straining to be released.

Reaching round, I find her entrance with my finger. Just as I expect, she's swollen, wet, and waiting for me.

"Hhmm." Katie pushes her clit into my fingers.

I pull away as she does. "Oh no, Kat-er-een. You have been a bad girl. You will have to wait for that."

A rattling on the door annoyingly brings me out of my domination.

"Go away," I boom.

"Boss. We have him. The car is ready." Van tries the door again. "The door is stuck."

"No, it is locked," I reply in frustration while squeezing the bottom of my wife.

"Why is it locked?"

"Because I am trying to fuck my wife. Now leave."

There's a giggle from Katie.

"It looks like you are getting away with it lightly tonight, Kat-er-een."

"I'll take whatever you've got, Mr Guerra."

After quickly opening my belt, I drop my pants and release my throbbing cock. I find her entrance with the tip and circle it lightly before I thrust into the heaven that is my wife.

After giving my wife a good seeing to and telling her I love her, I kiss my boys good night and get into the waiting car. As we drive through the Italian streets, I think about the life of crime to which we have returned and the laws that I am about to break, but in Italy, I am the law.

We pull up to one of our desolate warehouses. I walk to the building and am immediately let inside by my guards. I haven't met any of them before, but each gives a small nod of the head in respect. Respect which the Guerra has earned. Respect I have earned. Tonight, I need to remind people who I was and who I still am. The fact that I have a wife and children does not mean I have weakened. I still have the strength to lead the Guerra.

The room I am led into is dark and damp. The stench, a metallic mix of blood and disinfectant, is almost enough to make you throw up. One of the guards turns on a single light bulb that hangs from the high rafters above. A man, bloodied and beaten as I requested, remains slumped in the chair he is tied to.

"I heard you are the one who discovered I

was alive."

The man doesn't dare look up as I speak.

"You took an innocent woman's life even after she told you what you needed to know. Why was that?"

Her blood is partly on my hands. If I had not had such an outburst on the jet, she would never have disobeyed the restriction against entering my cabin. Her intentions were honourable in wanting to check I was okay. In return, she got shouted at by me and a death sentence.

"Did she submit to your interrogation immediately, or did you torture her first?"

This question wakens something inside him. He slowly raises his head, grinning evilly. "I had to get a bit rough with her first. But I think she enjoyed it."

Fury builds inside me. The whole crew was battered and questioned by the Martelé, but she was the only one who had been killed. She was the only one who had seen me and knew anything. Up until that point, the Martelé had no idea that I was alive. What they wanted to know was where Marco was, seeing as he was supposed to be dead but had somehow managed to kill their leader.

I approach the man while taking out my knife rather than my gun. A slower, more painful death is needed for this type of vermin.

"I absolutely despise men who abuse and hurt innocent women. You are nothing but a sewer rat who does not deserve to breathe the same air as me."

"Guerra scum." He spits.

And that's as much as I can take. With one hand, I grab his head and push it back, widening his neck. With the knife in my other hand, I automatically pierce the skin at one side of his throat and swipe quickly across in a single straight line. Blood spurts out, covering my suit. The disgusting middle-aged man gasps as blood fills his lungs. His eyes bulge in panic. I watch as he chokes and surrenders to death. It's a real nasty way to go. But he deserved it. I must show the new Guerra recruits why we are to be respected. I must show the Martelé that they cannot beat the Guerra.

Once the gurgling sounds have quietened and the rotten soul has left the man's body, I instruct Van to deliver it to the Martelé.

"Make it as messy as you can. Hang him from a tree or something like it."

"Do you want it to be discreet?"

"No, Van. I want the whole of Italy to know that I am back and that the Guerra mean business."

"What about the police?"

"Don't worry about the police."

In a few hours, the country will wake up to

the news that I have come back from the dead. Leo Guerra has been resurrected and he doesn't fuck around. The police have always been in the Guerra's pockets, apart from Lorenzo, the last Chief of Police, but I put a bullet in his head to remind them of what will happen if they dare to cross the Guerra again.

The car returns me home. After removing my clothes and taking a shower, I check on my boys, who are fast asleep. I then slide into bed behind my wife and take a deep breath. The smell of home. It's quite surreal being back here. Adrenaline pumps through my body. The night's activities run through my mind. I feel alive.

Leo Guerra is back.

Katie

When I wake, Leo is snuggled against my back. I can tell by his breathing that he is still fast asleep. I'm not sure what time he came in last night—well, early this morning—but I know I fed Zander at 3:00 a.m., and he wasn't back then. It's 7:00 a.m. now, and Zander is stirring, ready for his next feed.

I throw on my dressing gown and pick him up before he disturbs Leo. The door to Mark's room is slightly ajar, so I pop my head around it to check, and he is still fast asleep. I've got the baby monitor, so I go downstairs to make Zander his bottle. Alga and Sergio are already in the kitchen, preparing delicious-smelling food.

"Good morning, Mrs Guerra."

"Please, Alga, you always call me Katie."

Alga nods and smiles. "Good morning, Katie. What can I get for you?"

"A coffee would be great while I just get Zander's bottle ready."

"Already done. Here you are. Just check the temperature."

"Ahh, Alga, you are a star." I take the bottle as Sergio sets a cappuccino down on the island next to me. As soon as I'm comfy on a stool, I give Zander his bottle.

"Did you all sleep okay?" Alga asks.

"We did. I'm not sure what time Leo got in, but he is well away now."

Alga smiles. She would never comment on any of Leo's activities. "How do you like the baby monitor?" she asks, nodding at my dressing gown pocket, where it sticks out. "You know it has a two-way speaker and a playback function for the videos." She gives me a little wink, making me laugh.

It's great that I can check on everyone else, but I must remember to turn the one off in our room when we have mummy-and-daddy time.

"It's wonderful, thank you, Alga. You have thought of everything."

Alga's face is filled with emotion. She looks like she is about to cry.

I stand from my stool while still feeding Zander and move next to her, nudging her gently. "Hey, what's wrong?" As soon as the words leave my lips, her tears begin to flow.

"Ah Alga." Sergio groans and hands her a tissue. "I'm sorry about Alga." He apologises. "We are just so grateful you are back."

Alga sobs into her tissue. "I'm sorry." She leaves the room.

Sergio continues. "When you... *died,* it broke Alga's heart. I told her that it couldn't be true and that you would be living a wonderful life somewhere. She didn't believe it, and to be honest, neither did I. I just said that to console her."

"I'm so sorry, Sergio. We had no other option. It breaks my heart thinking about what we put everyone through." My thoughts go to my parents, who as far as I know still are unaware of our return. Leo wants to wait until everything is sorted with the Martelé, as they will want to see us as soon as they find out.

"Alga hasn't been well since you've been gone. But after Marco told us you are alive, have two little boys, and planned on coming home, it's like she has a new lease of life."

Alga returns. "I am okay now."

I pass Zander to Sergio and wrap my arms around Alga. "Missed you."

"I missed you too."

We stand for a moment in an embrace. I let her let go first.

"Come on, that's enough now," Sergio tells us. "You're upsetting the baby."

We aren't, but Sergio hands Zander back to me, looking relieved not to be holding a baby. The monitor alerts us to movement in Mark's room. On the cameras, I see him starting to stir.

"It looks like your big brother is waking up," I say to Zander.

"May I?" Alga asks, already making her way towards the door.

"Of course." I gesture for her to continue out of the room.

With Mark only having met Alga last night, I'm unsure of how he will react when he wakes in a strange room after only half the amount of sleep he usually does. But I shouldn't have worried. I watch the camera as Alga enters, a beaming smile on her face as she sings an Italian good morning song. Mark stands in his bed and dances along with her. He happily takes her hand and jumps down from his bed. They're soon downstairs, laughing together.

We have a lovely morning start around the kitchen island, eating breakfast, catching up on all that's happened since we left, and listening to Mark happily talk about himself. It's almost 11:00 a.m. when Leo enters the kitchen, fully dressed in his crisp white shirt and tailored suit.

"Papa! Look outside! There's a swimming pool!"

"Wow, look at that," Leo says as he kisses his cheek, and then he does the same to Zander, who is sleeping in my arms.

Alga has an emotional smile on her face as she watches his gestures.

"Will you play with me in the water?" Mark asks.

"Not today, son. But soon. Mummy will, though, won't you Mummy?"

Hearing Leo call me Mummy while dressed in full Guerra boss attire has me giggling. "Yes, Mummy will play with you. And maybe we could take Zander for his first swim too?"

"Oh yes! Yes!" Mark gives Zander a pat on his head and starts talking to him about swimming.

"Alga, would you watch them for a few minutes?"

Leaving the boys in the kitchen, I beckon Leo into his office and close the door behind us.

"So? What's happening? Do my parents know we are back?"

"Not yet. Let me get the surprise with Alex and the Martelé over with first, and then we will fly your parents over."

"When are you seeing the Martelé?"

"This evening. Alex and Vanna will arrive this afternoon. We will finalise negotiations first, and then the meeting will take place."

The worry has me taking a deep breath.

"Do not worry. Everything is in hand." Leo puts his hands on my folded arms. "Marco is on his way with Mia and Larisa. So be nice."

His remark makes me laugh. "I'm always nice."

When I first met Mia, I wasn't over keen. But once I realised it was Marco she wanted to get her claws into, I calmed down. From what I heard from Leo, Mia and Marco have had a really hard time. I now realise why Leo had to come back. He had no option.

"I better go and get dressed, then," I say.

Marco, Mia and Larisa arrive just as the boys

and I are ready. Marco is dressed in this three-piece suit looking his usual evil, grumpy self, but as soon as the petit dark-haired baby in his huge arms touches his face, his eyes light up and the dark expression cracks, revealing a loving father. It's a very surreal sight but one that melts my heart.

Mia looks as stunning as always in a bright red dress and gold-heeled sandals. "Katie, it's so good to see you."

And she genuinely looks pleased to see me, which makes me relax. She takes my hand and gives it squeeze, but I pull her in for a hug. She smells amazing, and her makeup is perfect. I do notice some scars on one side of her face. They must be from the car accident. They don't, however, effect how beautiful she is.

A boy's voice interrupts our greetings before a head pops around from Marco's back. "Hello."

"Alfie? Is that you?"

"Yep."

"Wow. Come here. Let me see you."

Alfie comes to stand in front of me, and he is almost as tall as I am.

"You got so big!"

"Emmaline had some errands to run, but she will be along shortly, so we brought Alfie," Mia explains. "I hope that's okay?"

"Of course. Come on in and let's go outside. Mark is dying to get in the swimming pool."

Everyone other than Marco follows me outside. He goes into the office to join Leo.

Alfie is a very welcome distraction for Mark. They play together in the pool, which leaves me to catch up with Mia. Both Zander and Larisa are asleep in their prams in the shade when Emmaline arrives. I'm not sure how I expected Emmaline to be when I first saw her, but it wasn't like this.

Emmaline was my best and only friend when I lived in Italy. I met her on the beach one day soon after I arrived. She was with Alfie and her dog Macy, and we connected straight away. Emmaline kept me sane. I don't know what I would have done without her. Mia and I are mid-conversation when Alga shows Emmaline where we are sat.

"Hi," Emmaline says as she sits in a chair opposite me, next to Mia.

"Hello," I reply, sitting back down, as it looks like I'm not getting a hug.

Mia looks at me with sympathy and takes a big sip of her drink. Alga interrupts the silence by bringing another jug of cocktails and a glass for Emmaline. They make small talk about Alfie and how much he has grown. Once it's just the three of us again, I have to break the ice, it's breaking my heart to look at Emmaline. She must be so angry with me. So hurt. I'm not sure how to approach it, so I go with my gut.

"Emmaline, are you okay?" I ask as sincerely as I can.

At first, she doesn't reply, just takes a sip of her drink and a deep breath. Although she is wearing sunglasses, I can tell by the cheeks around her eyes that she has been crying.

"Emmaline is struggling to deal with the news," Mia explains. "It was very hard for her when you *passed away*. Especially in the circumstances. Alfie didn't deal with it well either. It's taken a long time for both of them to come to terms with what happened."

A sob comes from Emmaline, and she takes a larger sip of her cocktail.

"Oh, Emmaline, I am so sorry." My heart hurts and tears fill my eyes. I can't help but go to her and wrap my arms around her. We both cry and squeeze each other tightly.

"Mum, are you okay?" Alfie shouts from the pool, noticing his mum upset.

"She's fine. Just happy. You carry on playing," Mia shouts back. "Right, come on you two. You're upsetting the children.

"Katie. What happened was fucked up. You broke everyone's hearts and left people with anxiety and depression. But if you hadn't killed yourselves, the Martelé would have done it anyway. Emmaline, you've got your friend back, for now anyway, and we all die at some point. So come on. Let's make the most of it and get pissed." Mia's bluntness makes us both laugh. And with what Mia and Marco have been through, I'm not surprised by her outlook on life.

We soon fall back into our comfortable friendly ways. We even have a swim in the pool. Then the babies decide they have had enough of the water, so Mia and I exit first, leaving Emmaline playing with the boys. The day has been full of laughter, and I have had the best time I've had in years. It's so nice to be around friends. I've really missed this.

When Emmaline does decide to get out of the pool, Alfie has other ideas. He grabs her by the arm and pulls her back in. Emmaline screams, trying to fight him off, but ends up in the pool again. Out of nowhere a large, suited man comes jumping into the pool. He grabs Emmaline and lifts her onto the side. Our laughter stops at this point, all in shock at what is going on.

"For god's sake," Mia shouts as she runs to the pool and grabs the collar of the man, who still hasn't resurfaced. From the edge, she pulls him to the steps. A very wet, fully suited Van emerges from the water, a little breathless.

"What the fuck is going on?" Leo booms, storming out of the house in our direction.

"I heard Emmaline screaming," Van splutters. "I jumped in to save her."

"But you can't fucking swim!" Mia slaps her brother on his arm.

"I don't think she needed saving, Van." Leo is cross.

Emmaline blushes as she looks at Van. "Thank you, Van, although Leo is right. We were just playing. Sorry you got wet."

Alfie bursts into laugher, and we all then join in on the hilarious sight of Van, dripping wet in a three-piece suit.

"Get inside and get changed. We've got work to do," Leo instructs Van as he turns on his heels and returns to the house.

Van follows, squelching with each footstep.

"Where did he even come from?" I laugh.

"Wherever Emmaline is, Van isn't far behind." Mia smirks.

"Cut it out. We are just friends." Emmaline flicks water from her hands at a dry Mia.

"Yeah, well, he's a dope anyway. You can do better than my brother."

"He is not a dope. But I don't want a man. I have Alfie, and he is the only boy I want in my life." Emmaline wraps a towel around herself.

"So there's still no romance in the air for you,

then, Emmaline?" I ask, having not touched on that part of her life in a while, or, come to think of it, ever.

"No. I've had enough bad experiences with men before Alfie was born to last me a lifetime. I am perfectly happy on my own, thank you."

Getting the message that Emmaline no longer wants to talk about her love life I lighten the mood again. "Can Van really not swim?"

"Nope. It's like he's made of steel or something. His body has real high density and just sinks."

We all have another laugh and finish the remainder of the cocktails.

"Well, well, well." Mia stands mid-conversation and removes her sunglasses.

Emmaline and I turn to see what she is looking at. Segio exits the house, followed by Alex and Vanna.

"Ladies." Sergio stands tall and professional. He gestures to our new arrivals. "Alessandro Guerra and his wife, Giovanna Guerra." He then bows his head to them and returns to the house.

Vanna removes her sunglasses, and I can see her looking Mia up and down, taking in her very revealing red swimsuit.

Alex and Vanna look like your stereotypical mafia boss and his wife. Vanna wears an oversized brown blazer cinched with a designer statement belt, a black leather skirt, barely there tights, and leopard-print stilettos. Her dark hair is twice the size I've ever seen it, styled in waves. Her lips are bright red, giving Mia a run for her money. She wears a death stare and is completely unrecognisable from the Vanna I know from Nuova Vita Island.

Alex wears a tailored black power suit, a statement that says, "I'm here to take over."

"Vanna, Alex, hi. It's so good to see you."

Vanna's face softens when she looks at me, but not enough that I feel like I can give her a hug, which I would have done without thinking a couple of days ago.

"This is Mia Guerra, Marco's wife. And Emmaline, a friend of ours."

"Hello, nice to me you." Emmaline gives them both a little wave while Mia struts over to them and shakes their hands whether they want to or not. I see Leo appear at the door. I watch him take a deep breath before he greets them.

"Alex, Vanna, you're here. Come, we are in the office," Leo says matter-of-factly and guides them into the house.

This all feels very strange.

"So, who are they, then?" Emmaline asks.

"That is Leo's brother. He was supposed to

be dead too. And that woman he is married to is a Martelé," Mia explains sternly.

Emmaline gasps.

"She's really nice once you get to know her," I fire back at Mia.

"She's a Martelé, Katie. They cannot be trusted." Mia wraps her robe around herself and gathers her things. "I'm going now. Larisa needs to get home. I'll call you both later."

Once Mia leaves, Emmaline and Alfie do, too, much to the protest of Mark. He has had the best day playing in the pool. He even missed his nap, so I'm hoping to get him to bed early, and he should sleep through.

Alga helps me bath the boys and get them ready for bed. There are a lot of Guerra men in the house coming and going for the meetings, so we spend the evening upstairs. We all have supper sitting on the floor like a picnic and watch cartoons. The boys are shattered after a busy day and are soon asleep after Leo popped his head in and wished them good night.

I, too, have my pj's on, and I'm looking forward to a peaceful night once the men leave for business. Hopefully tomorrow everything will be sorted, and we can start putting our life back together. But I should know better. When you are part of the Guerra, things don't always go as planned.

Leo.

"Enough!" I've had all I can take of Marco and Alex arguing.

Alex wants to take over the Martelé. He wants to control them. Marco wants nothing to do with them. He wants to irradicate them, not become part of them.

I have to agree with Marco. "We do not want the Guerra name to be associated with any of the types of dealings they involve themselves in. Guerra protect women and children, not traffic them.

"That is a minor detail and one that will be resolved once we take over. You need to look at the bigger picture," Vanna chirps in.

She surprises me with her lack of empathy. Maybe she is more Martelé than I first thought.

She continues, "That organisation is mine. I have it here in black and white." She puts the documents she's been holding down on the desk.

"And why would they just hand everything over?" Marco asks.

"Because upon my father's death, which you kindly carried out, Marco, all the estates, companies, and properties were left to me, the oldest child. They were only passed down to my brother because of my death. Which never happened. There is no death certificate, so everything is mine."

"The Martelé soldiers won't answer to you. You are a woman, for one."

Marco's statement earns a fist to the desk from my brother. "Do not disrespect my wife."

"They will have to, or they will answer to no one. Without the businesses, the property, the deals, the money, the Martelé have nothing."

She has a good point.

Marco still does not agree. "The Guerra cannot be seen to be involved with such disgusting acts. It is a disgrace to the name that has been built over generations. We will have dropped deals. Contacts will turn their backs."

"The Guerra will stay as they are. Vanna and I will take over the Martelé, and you and Leo will lead here. Nothing changes other than your death warrant."

Alex's revelation concerns me. He doesn't know what he is letting himself in for. But their decision has been made, and for now, I cannot argue. We will have to deal with the consequences when they happen. It's time we get to the meeting. Marco hasn't said another word. I'm sure he is thinking the same as I am.

"If that's what you want, so be it. Who is it we are meeting, Vanna?" I ask.

"My mother and her brother. They have taken over leadership until one of my cousins on my father's side is eighteen, or so they think."

"Wow, that will be an interesting family reunion. They still have no idea you are alive?" I ask, looking forward to seeing how this unfolds.

"Not a clue."

"Right. Get the cars ready, Van. I need one guard to stay here with my family. The rest will come with us. They will wait outside, do pat-downs, and collect all firearms and weapons before anyone enters. They need to be ruthless. Anyone who disobeys, they kill them on the spot. We need to show them we mean business. Who do you trust the most, Van?" I ask, as Van has done most of the recruiting.

"Oh, Vine, definitely," he answers instantly.

Once I've said goodbye to my wife and children, I find the guards waiting in the hallway.

"Vine?" I call out, and one steps forward. He's an ugly beast of a man who doesn't smell the best.

"Boss."

"You will stay here and look after my family.

The rest will follow in the cars behind us. Van will give your instructions on the way."

I'm apprehensive about leaving my world behind again. But they will be safe in the house with a guard that Van trusts. A few hours and I will be back.

When we arrive at our mutually chosen location, myself, Marco, Alex, and Vanna wait in the car while the guards check the safety of the building and do their pat-downs. Only five members from each organisation are allowed in the meeting. When our guards have retrieved the weapons from the Martelé, they enter, and we exit the car and receive the same treatment from the Martelé. The Martelé guards give snide remarks when they see me alive and well. They do not comment on Alex or Vanna. They clearly don't recognise them after all these years.

Van, Marco, and I enter the disused restaurant first, with Alex and Vanna following close behind us but out of their line of sight.

Vanna's mother and uncle face us, sat at a large round table with three men stood behind them. Van introduces us on entry as Leonardo Guerra and Marco Guerra.

"We know who you are," Vanna's mother spits. "You should have stayed dead. We will come for you and your little family. Both of you. We will murder your children while you and your wives watch, and then we will kill you." Vanna's uncle adds.

Marco lunges forward, but I put an arm out to stop him. Each member of the Martelé laughs.

"You killed my husband and my son. Do you really think I will let you live?"

"Your husband was a sick, twisted man, and he deserved to die. Your son raped and trafficked women. He deserved more than death."

Vanna's uncle stands, banging his fists on the table. "Enough. What is it you want, Guerra, or have you just come to gloat?"

"We have come to take over your organisation," Marco states matter-of-factly.

More laughter comes from the Martelé. We stand in silence and wait for them to finish.

Vanna's mother stands. "We have torn down the Guerra before, and we will do it again. Stop joking around and get to the point, or we are leaving."

Alex speaks from behind me. "We have come to take over."

"Who are you? Make yourself known," Vanna's uncle protests.

Alex and Vanna walk out from behind us.

"Hello, Mother. Bea Martelé."

I watch as the reality hits Vanna's mother,

Bea. It takes her a moment, and there's a strong frown on her face as her eyes settle on Vanna's. She gasps, putting her hands over her mouth, and sinks back into her chair. Tears stream from her face. "It can't be."

"Uncle Joe," Vanna greets her uncle coldly. "He's not the only one who can come back from the dead." She gestures in my direction.

"You!" Vanna's mother looks at Alex and stands again angrily. "You took her away."

"No, you all pushed me away. Dad had him killed. Well, almost. Luckily my husband is made of tough stuff."

"Your husband?" Uncle Joe growls in protest. "You married a Guerra."

"Yes. Now that the introductions are over, I'd like to get down to business." Alex pulls up a chair at the table, and Vanna takes a seat. Alex stands behind her and passes her the documents, which she places on the table in front of them.

"'My final will and testament...'" Vanna begins to read her father's will and the conditions upon which he has left everything to her on his passing.

"Is this some kind of joke? You don't think you can just walk in here and take over everything." Uncle Joe laughs.

Vanna's mother picks up the documents and

slumps back in her seat while reading, the penny dropping, Vanna's words clearly hitting hard. "It's true," she says.

Uncle Joe snatches the documents from her hands, rips them up, and throws them back at Vanna. "You have nothing. For all we know, you are an imposter. And even if you are Vanna, you are a Guerra now. Guerra cannot be Martelé."

"I am still a Martelé. It just doesn't mean the same as it used to."

"Well, you are married to a Guerra. Our men will never work under your control."

The guards behind him nod and grunt in agreement.

"Oh, but you see, Uncle, my husband married me, so he is a Martelé."

Alex quickly picks Vanna up just as the table is thrown by her uncle. Marco, Van, and I quickly step into action, standing between Vanna and her uncle, whose guards are also stood beside him, ready for action.

"Vanna. My daughter. This is too much." She cries.

Vanna moves us out from behind us to stand in front of her mother, uncle, and the guards.

"I am Giovanna Martelé. The organisation was left to me when my father was murdered. This is my birthright, my destiny. I am the heir, the last of the true immediate bloodline. You will bow to me."

"Never!" Uncle Joe shouts and lunges for Vanna, but this time, it's the Martelé guards that get to Vanna first, grabbing her uncle by the arms and throwing him to the floor.

"How dare you lay your hands on me. You will pay for that!" Joe shouts.

"Oh, but they won't." Vanna nods in thanks to the guards.

Van appears from behind me and hands Vanna a bag.

She takes it and reaches inside. "Here are your phones. If you'd like to check your bank balances, I think you will find it very interesting."

Both of Vanna's relatives take their phones, as do the guards. After a moment, the guards look very pleased with what they see, showing one another their devices.

"I can't get on it. It says 'account suspended.'" Bea continues to put in her password as though it might change.

"Mine too."

"Yes, dear uncle—yours too. Both of your accounts have been closed. Your access to all of the Martelé businesses, legit and underworld, have been terminated. You have nothing. Guards, you have been paid a well-overdue bonus. Every worker has. If you comply with the future changes, you will again be compensated and continue to be while working under my reign," Vanna continues.

Marco and I look at each other. I had no idea the takeover was already in progress. This must have been what Alex and Vanna wanted to sort out before they came. I'm annoyed I wasn't told about this before we came. I thought it would be Alex making all the decisions and that he was the one who I would have my work cut out with, but it looks like it's actually Vanna who is pulling all the strings. Vanna is taking over the Martelé as a Martelé, and my brother is at her side. I cannot get my head around what is happening.

"Vanna, please, can I speak to you alone?" her mother asks gently.

"No. You cannot. I will be arranging meetings with each of you, but at my convenience. For now, you can return to your homes. But I own the houses, and I will be using them how I decide."

"Bitch!" Uncle Joe goes for her again, and this time he is met with crack to the face by a Martelé guard. He drops to his knees, holding his face. It looks like Vanna has them under her control already.

"Make no mistake. This is happening, and unless I have your complete cooperation, you will be out, completely cut off. I'll give you twenty-four hours to get your head around it or to try and find a way to stop me, which you can't. Then we will meet back here, and I will go through my plans."

The Martelé guards help Uncle Joe to his feet and escort him and Vanna's mother out of the building.

When they have gone, Vanna breathes a sigh of relief, and her persona relaxes slightly. I'm still in shock over what I have just witnessed. The Vanna I have seen here tonight is a completely different version of the one I met on the island.

"You were amazing." Alex kisses Vanna's head.

"Hold on a minute. What the fuck was that?" Marco booms. "Why were we not told this information before we came?"

"We weren't sure how we were going to play it. But when I saw my uncle and mother and how they reacted, I thought, fuck it, I'm taking it all."

"So, you are now the head of the Martelé, our arch enemy?" Marco scoffs.

"Yes, Marco I am." Vanna smirks proudly.

What the hell is going on here?

"Scotch, anyone?" Van asks. He has a habit of appearing out of nowhere.

"Give me that." Marco takes the bottle from his hand and grabs a glass from a nearby cabinet. He pours himself a shot, downs it, then pours himself another and downs that too. "What are these plans that you are going to go through with them tomorrow?" Marco is very agitated. He doesn't like not being kept in the loop. It makes him not trust people.

"How the structure will change, what deals we will be terminating, and the different connections we will now be working with."

"Connections, what connections?" I ask, confused as to how they have any new connections. It seems Katie was right. Alex may be my brother, but I do not know him or his wife at all. "Actually, don't answer that. I've had enough surprises for one day. Come on, Marco. Let's go home."

Van appears again out of the darkness. "There's some trouble outside. Don't leave yet."

"What kind of trouble?" I groan, hoping this doesn't delay my return home.

"Some of the Martelé guards that were doing the searches got a bit arsey when I was giving them their weapons back. I need Vine to teach them a lesson."

"Can't you just shoot him yourself?" Marco inquires.

"I could, but Vine does scary sick things that will haunt their nightmares for years."

Hold on a minute. I know that name. "Vine?"

"Yes. Have you seen him?"

"Yes, I left him at the house with my wife and children."

"Why would you do that?" Van asks, concern filling his face.

"Because I asked you who you could trust, and you said Vine."

"Yeah, trust to be ruthless and kill someone on the spot, not trust anywhere near women and children. Fuck, he ripped out a man's voice box with his teeth. He is an actual monster." Van physically shudders.

My heart pounds in my chest. I look at Marco, who already has his phone in his hand. He dials, but it rings out. I check the house cameras. Nothing. Nobody is in any of the rooms. The only rooms the cameras aren't in are ours and Mark's room, which has the baby monitor. That monitor, I do not have on my phone.

"Shit," I say. "Get in the car now."

We all get into the car. It's about a twenty-minute drive away. Each of us tries Katie's phone, the house phone, and Alga and Sergio, who live on the grounds. There's no answer on any of them. Van tries Vine, but it goes straight to answer phone.

"I'm sure they will all be fine, Leo," Van assures me. "They're probably all just asleep. It is almost ten o'clock."

"They better be. I cannot believe you, Van. How could you say you trusted him? if anything has happened to them, I will be holding you responsible!"

I know it's not Van's fault, but at this moment in time, I am angry—mostly with myself for leaving my family in danger again. They may well all be fine, but the familiar tug in my gut tells me that something is wrong.

"I've got Sergio." Marco holds his phone to his ear.

"Pass him to me." I take the phone from Marco. "Sergio, where are you?"

"Sorry, sir, I'm at home. I was asleep. Alga is still at the house."

"Where are Katie and the boys?"

"They were in bed when I left the house about an hour ago. Asleep, I presume, as they remained upstairs after you had gone."

"Where is Vine, the guard?"

"Oh, that angry-looking guard dog? He was patrolling the grounds when I left."

"I need you to get back to the house, lock all the doors, and do not let Vine into the building. We are on our way back now."

"I'll return immediately. Are they in danger?

Alga is still at the house, finishing the laundry."

"Hopefully not. Just lock the doors and tell Vine I have requested that he keeps a lookout on the grounds and not to enter the house. In fact, tell him to answer his fucking phone!"

"Will do, boss. I'm leaving now."

"Ring me as soon as you are in the house." I end the call.

Chapter Twelve

Katie

After the boys have been asleep for a while, I feel tired myself, so I also get into bed.

My thoughts go to Leo. I hope everything gets sorted with the Martelé. I don't want to have to live in fear for the rest of my life. I know there will always be risks with Leo being who he is, but if we don't have a death warrant hanging over our heads, I will feel a lot better.

Although I am incredibly tired, I just can't sleep. After checking the boys are okay, I go downstairs and find Alga in the laundry room. It's a large room with two industrial-size washing machines and tumble dryers. There is one on each side of the room. On the left side, they are white, and those are what I use whenever I'm washing our clothes. On the opposite side are black machines. These are strictly for work clothes. I've seen the mess some of the clothes are in when they go into those machines, and I'm grateful we have separate ones. Alga is at the back of the room, steaming some white shirts. She is the reason all the Guerra men look so pristine.

"Alga," I call, making her jump a little. "Sorry, I didn't mean to sneak up on you."

"Oh, Katie dear, I was in a world of my own." Alga takes so much pride in her work. She's like everyone's mother, ensuring everyone is looked after. "I thought you were all asleep."

"I'm really tired, but I couldn't settle."

"Come on, I'm finished here now. Let's have a cup of tea." Alga puts her hand gently on my back and leads me into the kitchen.

"Shouldn't you be getting to bed? It's very late," I say as she puts on the kettle, and I get the cups out of the cabinet.

"Oh, I don't need much sleep these days. I'd rather be up doing things. There'll be plenty of time to sleep when I'm dead." She chuckles while putting the teabags in the cups.

"I know, but you mustn't do too much. I don't know what any of us would do without you, so you must look after yourself." I make a mental note to myself to speak to Leo about not working her so hard. I know we've been away for years, but she has aged a lot and looks much thinner than she used to.

"Thank you. But honestly, I'm fine. I'll have this drink, then get off. Now, you tell me all about little Zander and Mark. What was he like as a baby?" We sit down at the table with our drinks.

"When we had Mark, we were living in a little bubble. It feels like a dream now, thinking back. I had found out I was pregnant not long after arriving at the island, and we were so happy. I had the perfect pregnancy, Leo was so protective of me, doing everything. He wouldn't let me lift a finger. The birth was perfect, a quick natural delivery with Leo by my side the whole time, unlike Zander's." I continue to explain how perfect the start of Mark's life was, leaving the trauma of Zander's delivery for another time.

"We lived in a lovely family home that Leo and I renovated ourselves, and Leo had the grounds turned into orchards and beautiful gardens. On our first anniversary there, Leo bought me some chickens, something I had always wanted. Our days were filled with family time, walking on the beautiful beaches, and spending time in our home. Mark had both his mummy and papa with him 24/7, and as parents we did everything fifty-fifty. Leo is an amazing father."

Alga's face is full of pride. She has always thought of him as more than a boss.

After about half an hour of me talking about our time on the island and Alga thoroughly enjoying every word, I say, "I'm feeling tired now. I think I'll go back to bed." More for Alga's benefit really. I want her to get some rest because I know she will be back here at the crack of dawn.

"Yes, you get off to bed. I'll just finish a couple of things in the laundry room, and then I'll get to bed too."

"Well, don't be long. You work too hard." I kiss Alga good night on the cheek and go back to my room.

When I return to our bedroom, I feel like something is off. I check on Zander, who is still fast asleep in his cot beside our bed. Then I notice that the door that joins Mark's room to ours is closed. I'm sure I left it open. I always do, so that if he wakes in the night, he can find his way to us.

I quickly open his door and enter his room, which is in complete darkness now lit only by the dim light coming from our room. Again, I'm certain I left Mark's night light on.

When I reach Mark's bedside, I thankfully find him still asleep. Sitting with him a moment, I stroke his head, trying to work out what might have happened. Maybe in my tiredness, I turned out his light and shut the door. It's the only explanation, as it's only me and Alga in the house, and Alga is downstairs. But there's a tug in my gut that just won't let my brain explain it away. When I'm happy Mark is content, I leave his side and switch on his night light.

That is when I notice the eyes.

Wide eyes staring at me, watching my every move.

A gasp escapes my lips.

A chill runs down my body.

A very large, haunted-looking man stands in Mark's bedroom by the door.

"Wh-what are you doing in h-here?" I demand, stumbling over my words.

But the man just stares at me intimidatingly.

"You need to leave. You shouldn't be in here."

I'm sure he is one of the Guerra guards. In fact, I recognise him now as one of the guards who met us off the plane. I remember his cold stare. Still there is no response.

"Get out!" I scream in panic, emotion filling my voice.

This gets a slight smirk in response. "I will be leaving soon. But I will be taking your son."

I feel sick. I rush forward to stand between him and Mark. "You are not taking my son anywhere."

The smirk on his face grows. "Yes. I am."

"Get out now, while you still can. Leo will be home soon, and he will kill you for being in here."

There's slight amusement in his tone when he says, "Leo is on his way back. But they won't be here in time."

Standing firmly, I think of my options. I don't know whether there is a gun or weapon up here. I don't even have my phone with me. All the guards have gone apart from this one. Although, I think there will be someone at the gated entrance. Then I feel the baby monitor in my pocket. That could help. It has a two-way voice control. If I can switch it on, there may be a chance Alga is still here. She might hear it and then alert someone.

With his terrorising stare that hasn't left me for a moment, I know he will notice me fumbling around in my dressing gown pocket. I need to turn around and distract him.

"You are not taking my son." I say firmly as I turn and get on the bed next to Mark. Quickly, I put my hand in my pocket and turn on the button, praying I've pressed the right one.

When I turn back to look at him, he makes me jump with how close he his. My face is met with the barrel of a gun.

"Please don't take my son. Please just leave. Get out of my son's room. Please don't hurt my baby." I scream everything I tell him, hoping that the monitor picks it up.

Unfortunately, my loudness starts to wake Mark. I do not want him waking up to this nightmare. It will scar him for life. Wrapping my body around him so he can't see the horrifying reality of what's happening in his room, I start to sing his favourite nursery rhymes as gently and happily as a I can to settle him back to sleep. Thankfully, he does, but unfortunately the nightmare still continues. I can feel the presence of the man close behind me.

When I turn to look at him, he has a confused expression on his face.

"Please just leave us alone," I beg.

And then his smirk returns. "I will when you hand over your son."

"Never," I cry, holding on to my first baby.

"I will take the other one, then." He goes to leave the room.

"No!" I cry, leaving Mark and sprinting to the door to stand in his way. Standing firm, I try and act strong, but my emotion takes over and my words again come out in a cry. "You will not be taking either of my sons anywhere."

Now he begins to laugh. "Do you really think you can stop me?"

He pushes past me, throwing me to the floor. I scramble up instantly, fighting my way to Zander in the other room.

Again he laughs at my desperate actions. "You choose. This one..." He points his gun at Zander.

My chest becomes tight, and a wail leaves my throat. "No!" I cry.

"Or that one?" He points his gun at Mark's door.

My heart is racing, and I'm starting to feel dizzy. I need to protect my children. I need help. "Please!" I beg and slump to my knees, not knowing what else to do other than pray help arrives soon.

"I will take the older one." He moves back towards Mark's door.

I instantly dive towards him and grab on to his leg. He bursts into laugher again, watching me trying to stop his huge, heavy frame. He continues to walk, my attachment making no restriction to his movements.

Out of the corner of my eye, I see Alga at the door. Hoping she can read the situation, I continue to hang on to his leg and let him pull me into Mark's room. If she can get Zander out of the picture, I can try and protect Mark.

Once we are in Mark's room, I scramble up and fight him, using every bit of strength I have. I'm trained in self-defence. I have been taught how to use someone's strength against them. I perform a palm heel strike to his face. He is shocked by my strength—I can see it in his face. But it's not enough. Unfortunately, with him being so much taller than me, I couldn't get enough power behind the blow.

I then give him a front kick to his groin. It definitely hurts him, so I take the opportunity to go for his gun. I grab his arm at the wrist, spin the gun away from me, then kick him again in the groin. He buckles a little, but he doesn't let go. An almighty roar then leaves his throat. Standing tall again, he grabs me by the throat with his other hand, making me instantly let go of his arm. My hands go to his in an attempt to release his tight grip. He lifts me almost off the ground by my neck. I'm panicking from the lack of oxygen. I can't breathe.

He then slams me into the nearby wall and presses the barrel of the gun into my temple. "I will kill you first and then take both of them. Or you behave, and I let you and one of your sons live." His face is pure evil when speaks.

I can't reply. I'm seconds away from passing out. My eyes glaze over with tears of absolute fear for my children. Just before I fall unconscious, he releases my neck. I drop to the floor. My chest expands instantly, fighting for oxygen. My adrenaline kicks in, and I'm up on my feet while coughing and gasping for air. On unstable legs and with blurry vision, I force myself to get to Mark.

The vile man laughs at my efforts. But then stops. His attention perks up, and his eyes dart to the door. From our room, we hear Zander let out a little cry. The man storms to the door, and I just hope Alga has gotten away or that someone else is here.

"Stop right there!" The evil man demands when he exits Mark's room and continues into ours.

I follow him, and my heart sinks when I see Alga still in there with Zander in her arms, rushing to get away.

"Put him down, or I will shoot both of them!"

Alga stops, but she doesn't turn around. She holds Zander to her chest.

I can barely hold it together as a gun is pointed at my son. My breathing is erratic and panicked. All I can do is beg. "Please, kill me. Just don't harm my babies, please."

Slowly he turns to me, pointing the gun at my head. His face again has a wicked smile. Tilting his head to the side, he says, "I will kill you, and then I will take them both."

Alga takes the chance and runs to the door. But his reactions are faster. He shoots in their direction. I hear Alga drop to the floor.

The noise pierces my ears as much as the pain explodes in my heart. "My baby."

Another shot is fired. Now I hear Zander cry. He is still alive. I look in desperation. Alga is on her knees, hunched over Zander. Dark crimson fills her white blouse. She tries desperately to move. The vile guard just watches her as if he enjoys her struggle. Taking the opportunity, I quickly push myself up and dive on to him with as much strength as I can. Astonishingly I manage to knock him off balance. In his moment of distraction, I caught him off guard. Fighting with all my might, I try to wrestle the gun from his hands.

"Alga?"

Sergio's voice fills me with some hope.

"Sergio, quickly, please." But in my hope, I lose focus, then I'm overpowered and thrown across the room as he stands.

When I look in the direction of the door, Sergio has hold of Zander and disappears into the hallway. Alga lies lifeless on the floor. Again, I throw myself at the guard, grabbing on to his shirt, begging and pleading for him to leave my children alone. But I am no match for him.

He turns quickly, throwing an elbow to my face, and I drop to the floor. My head then is met by his boot. There's a sharp piercing crack as my eyes blur. *No, stay awake, Katie. You must stay awake and save your children.* Rolling onto my front, I push myself up, trying to get on to my knees. My heart sinks as I watch him leave the room, and I hear another loud, sharp, explosive sound that is becoming all too familiar.

"Mummy."

Mark's voice has my stomach turning. He cannot see this nightmare. I quickly run into his room, lift him out of bed, and put him in his wardrobe. "We are going to play a game, okay? Like hide and seek." I speak swiftly and clearly. Mark's tired eyes try and focus on me in the darkness. "You hide in here and don't come out until either me, Papa, or someone you know finds you. Okay? Can you do that for Mummy?"

Mark rubs his eyes and nods. I grab his iPad and headphones off his bedside table. "You can watch *In the Night Garden* while you wait." Thankfully Mark is happy with this. I quickly cover his ears and turn the volume up high. I close the door and pray he doesn't come out. I then return to the other room just as the evil man does.

Chapter Thirteen

Leo

"Sergio's not answering his phone. Why is he not answering his phone? He should be in the house by now."

"He is probably just checking on everyone before he does. Look, we are here now. Calm down."

"Don't tell me to calm down, Marco. If this was your fucking wife and child, you would be ripping Van's head off by now."

Marco is quiet, knowing full well I am right.

The car pulls up to the gates.

"Anything to report?" Van asks the guard as he lowers his window, waiting for the gates to open.

"No, all quiet, boss." He nods at me in the back.

When the gates are open far enough, Van sets off down the gravel driveway. But just before his window closes, I hear a sound I am very accustomed to in the direction of the house.

Marco looks at me with a concerned frown.

"Put your foot down, Van," I demand.

He instantly floors the accelerator. Stones fly up at the car with the spin of the wheels. I am out of the car before it has even stopped. Marco follows closely behind me. We both remove our guns from our belts and enter the house just as another shot is fired. I stop, holding my arm up to stop Marco.

"Our bedroom," I whisper just as Van joins us. "Go round the back, and get up on the balcony."

Marco nods.

"Van, with me. Do not make a sound."

We make our way up the stairs as discreetly as possible. Although my body fights the slow advance, I know the best chance I have of saving my family is with the element of surprise. The sound of my wife's voice fills my ears. I can't quite make out what she says, but I feel the pain in her voice. My chest compresses. But I push my emotions down. Gun at the ready, I'm on high alert, prepared to destroy the person who has brought this terror into my home.

As soon as we reach the top step, Sergio appears, running desperately from our bedroom. In his arms is my youngest son. He looks relieved to see me. He runs towards us. I hear the sound of heavy footsteps behind him. I beckon him to move faster. My strides are long and fast as I race to meet him. But I'm too late. A shot is fired. Sergio stops in his tracks. I see the life leave his eyes.

I catch my son before he falls from his arms, holding Sergio upright with my body as I swing my arm around him and fire.

My eyes meet Vine's. I missed. He wears an amused smirk. Instead of firing back, he retreats to the bedroom.

I pass Zander to Van. "Get him out." I lay Sergio on the floor.

On entering my bedroom, I find Vine holding my wife in front of him. He presses his gun at her temple with force while using her body to shield his. I notice Alga lying on the floor by my feet. A pool of blood surrounds her. There's a pang in my chest, but I will have to deal with it later.

"Let go of my wife!" I demand while pointing my gun, trying to find a clear shot.

Vine laughs. "Do you really think you can shoot me without blowing your wife's brains out all over your bedroom wall?"

"What do you want, Vine?"

"I want your family."

"Over my dead body!" I boom. But my words give me an idea.

The man is clearly a sadist. He receives pleasure from inflicting pain, humiliation, and suffering on others.

"That can be arranged." Vine laughs. He then whispers something into my wife's ear.

She cries out, "No. Please!"

He laughs again and nestles his face into her neck, rubbing his lips against her fast pulse.

The sight makes my blood boil. I want to blow his head off, but I know as soon as I pull the trigger, he will pull his, and she will be gone from my life forever. He continues exploring her neck with his tongue, enjoying her suffering—so much so he relaxes the hand that holds his gun. The barrel is now pointing upwards towards the ceiling.

I keep my eyes fixed on Katie's, hoping to give her strength and comfort. But as she calms, he becomes more alert, strengthening his grip, and the gun regains its position at her temple.

Finally, I see Marco behind them at the balcony window. He points his gun at Vine. He has a clear shot, but while Vine's gun is at my wife's temple, the shot is too risky.

Knowing what I need to do, I put my gun to my head. "Let my family go, and I will kill myself."

"Leo, no. What are you talking about? Please no!"

Vine is shocked by my suggestion, but I can see his pleasure build with my wife's horror.

"I'll shoot myself if you let them live."

"Leo, no. You can't trust him. Please, don't!" Katie cries.

"You wouldn't do it," Vine growls and wraps his teeth around my wife's neck.

My thoughts go to what Van said earlier, that he ripped out a man's throat with his teeth. I can no longer stand to watch this vile man touch my wife, so I fire my gun into my body. I pull the trigger, feeling the piercing pain rip through my skin—a pain that is almost as bad as the pain that pounds in my chest at watching my wife suffer.

Chapter Fourteen

Katie

The feel of this grotesque man's mouth on my neck has me shivering with revulsion. I close my eyes, trying to escape the nightmare that is my reality, in which my husband is saying he will take his life in return for ours. But I know this man would not let me and my boys go if Leo were to do that.

A shot is fired in front of me, and I know it was from Leo's gun. My scream comes out choked from my lungs. I cannot breathe. My chest restricts, and I buckle forward, my legs giving way. I hang loosely over the man's arm, still restrained. I feel him groan in pleasure at my pain. The gun releases from my head, but he still bites my neck painfully.

How could Leo do this? How could he leave me and our boys still in this hell and torture? Another shot is fired. My body plummets to the floor. The heavy weight of the man crushes me from behind. I lie there waiting for his next move, for him to strangle me, smash my head into the floor, anything. But it doesn't come. And then I hear it. The muffled voices around me become clear, and my heart feels like it begins to beat again.

"Get him off her!" Leo. His voice is like music to my ears. The weight is removed from my back, and I'm lifted into the arms of my husband. Relief fills me.

"I thought you were dead." My words come out as a cry.

"I'm sorry. I'm so sorry." Leo's stride has a limp as he walks us over to the bed and sits down. He cradles me into his chest, his mouth resting on the top of my head while he rocks slightly.

"Is he dead?" I ask, not wanting to look up.

"Yes."

"Mummy?"

Oh no. Both Leo and I jump up and dash to Mark's bedroom. Thankfully Mark is still in his wardrobe, just peeping through the door.

"Found you," I say through tears, trying to be as cheery as I can. "Well done Mark, you did so well."

I pick him up and take him to his bed. I climb in beside him.

Leo closes his bedroom door.

"Oh no, Papa, your foot!" Mark points to

Leo's limp. Small spots of blood stain the white carpet where Leo steps.

"I've just stepped on something sharp. Don't worry, buddy. I'll get a plaster on it soon. You go back to sleep."

I cuddle up to Mark and Leo covers us both. He kisses Mark and then me. "Stay here while I go and help clear up.

"Zander?" I sit up quickly, panicking.

"He's fine. He's with Van. I'll go and check on him."

"Mummy, what's wrong?"

"Nothing. I'm fine. I just thought I heard Zander crying, but Papa is going to check on him, and I will stay here with you."

Holding my son while he falls asleep feels like the most special thing in the world. I will never take these moments for granted. Children are precious. My heart pings with thoughts of what might have happened, how the night could have been heartbreakingly different. I stay in my little bubble with Mark until I hear the familiar sounds of his little snore, and I gently make my way out of his bed. I need to see Zander and check he is okay.

When I reach his door handle, I suddenly freeze. Alga. The last time I was in our room, her body lay lifeless on the floor. She has given her life for my children, for me.

"Sergio." His name leaves my mouth in a quiet gasp as I think about what he must be feeling.

I take a deep breath and prepare myself for what comes next. When I open the door, I am surprised to see the room empty. The carpets are gone, the furniture all removed. All that is in the room are two cleaners, who are disinfecting the floors and walls.

Leo appears in the doorway. "Is he asleep?"

"Yes. Where's Zander?"

"In the spare bedroom with Van. I'll carry Mark in there too."

Leo goes into Mark's room, carefully picks him up from his bed, and carries him down the hallway and into another bedroom. Zander is in the corner in his cot with Van stood on alert by his side.

Leo places Mark in the middle of the large bed. "We will all sleep in here until things are resolved."

Zander is peaceful with not a scratch on him. I say a little prayer in gratitude for my children and kiss his head.

"I need to see Sergio to thank him for saving Zander and to…. Well, tell him about Alga." Emotion overtakes my words.

Van clears his throat to speak, but Leo interrupts.

"Van, you stay in here. Guard my children with your life. One foot wrong, and you will be the next body in a body bag downstairs, do you hear me?!" Leo abruptly growls under his breath to not wake the children.

He puts his hand lightly on my back leads me out of the room. "I'm afraid Sergio was also caught in the firing line. He got Zander to safety, but unfortunately was shot and killed by Vine.

"No." My heart rips. Tears uncontrollably stream from my eyes. My legs buckle. There's a ringing in my ears.

Leo supports my weight as he leads me down the stairs and into the kitchen, which is bustling with people.

Mia is the first to greet me. "Katie." She pulls me into a hug. My body doesn't respond back. I'm in shock. "I'm so glad you are all right. The boys— are they okay? Did they see anything?"

"Both are sleeping, Mark woke up. But I hid him in the wardrobe." My reply is robotic. I'm now numb. I cannot believe they are gone. They saved my babies and gave their own lives.

"Here, come this way." Leo guides me away from Mia, who had continued to talk with no response from me. "I want you checked out by the medics."

It's like I'm outside of my body, looking down on myself as I get my blood pressure taken and monitors stuck to my chest. The kitchen is full of people. Marco and Mia and Alex and Vanna are here as well as guards and cleaners and other people whom I have no clue about, but they rush around, and the sound is just a constant hum. The whole situation, although vivid in my mind, just doesn't seem real. Part of me thinks this is just a horrendous nightmare and I will wake up from a nap on the beach with Leo and Mark paddling happily in the sea.

"Mrs Guerra? Mrs Guerra?" The medic pulls me back into my conscious mind.

"Sorry?"

"I said your heart rate is over one hundred, and your blood pressure is extremely high. I need to put you on some medication to bring it down, and then you need to rest."

I hadn't realised Leo was standing beside me. "I'm on it," he says as he picks me up.

"Leo, your foot?" I remind him feeling the slight limp as he walks me out of the kitchen.

"It's just a flesh wound. I'm fine." We walk past Marco on the way to the stairs, and Leo tells him, "Take care of this shit show. I'm taking my wife to bed."

When we get to the bedroom where our boys lie sleeping, we find Van pacing up and down the room between them like some sort of King's Guard. He stops when we enter.

"We are going to bed. Sit outside the room until morning."

Van nods at Leo's request and hurries out of the room, closing the door behind him.

"Why are you being so off with Van?"

"Because he is the most mindless imbecile I have ever met. If there was an award for stupidity, he wouldn't even win it because he would be too dumb to enter."

His reply would normally amuse me, but tonight I feel numb. Leo and I shower together to wash off the night. He cleans me gently while I stand with my head bowed, deep in thought. He brushes my hair and helps me get dressed before putting me to bed. Once he's redressed the wound on his foot, he cuddles up behind me.

"Ti amo," he whispers into my neck. *I love you.*

The next morning, Mark wakes up excited to find we are all sleeping in the same bed. "I didn't know we were having a sleepover!"

His innocence makes my heart swell but break at the same time. Zander also starts to stir, ready for a feed, so Leo and I get up and chat to our boys as if everything is perfectly normally.

I'm apprehensive to leave the bedroom, but I need not have been. Other than Van, who is stood outside our bedroom door, the house is like nothing has happened. We walk past our bedroom, and there is a new carpet in there, and all the furniture has been put back. Downstairs is as immaculate as always, but there's no smell of freshly baked pastries or coffee, and it feels very empty.

"Where's Alga?" asks Mark, having taken to her so fondly in such a short space of time.

I look to Leo to respond, as I'm not sure I can talk without getting emotional.

"They've gone on holiday. Now, what would you like for breakfast? I think we have some cereal around here somewhere." Leo checks the cupboards.

"Where have they gone?" Mark pushes.

Leo turns to Mark. "They've gone to a very nice place like where we used to live. They are together and will be happy there."

"Oooh, they should go to the beach."

"That is a wonderful idea. You know there is a beach here. Shall we go today?" Leo asks, changing the subject.

After breakfast and I've been checked over

by the medic again, we get ready and go to the beach. I'm glad to be out of the house and back on the beach that I know and love. We sit in our old spot with our backs to the rocks with a view in all directions. Zander is sat happily in his pram in the shade, and Mark plays excitedly in the sand.

Then Leo surprises me. "Your parents are on their way. Their plane lands in one hour."

My breath is taken with excitement but also dread. "What do they know?"

"They have been told we are alive and that we have sent for them. Your father isn't convinced, but Marco is escorting them and wouldn't take no for an answer."

Tears flood my eyes as my body lets me once again become emotional. "What should I tell them? How do I explain?"

Leo wipes the tears from my checks and takes both of my hands in his. "Tell them the truth."

"And what is the truth, Leo? What happens now? What will our future look like now we are back? I can't go through last night's torture again. I just can't."

"What do you want our future to look like, Kat-er-een?"

"Well, I want a *future,* for starters. A future with my boys, and one that doesn't involve having their lives threatened." I shudder as I think of anything happening to them. "I want a close family life. A normal family home. Not one that has separate washing machines for blood and guts. I want just one washing machine and one dryer. I want Mark to have his billy goats and me to have my chickens."

"I think we can manage that," Leo agrees, to my surprise.

"How? How can we have any of that if you are the leader of the Guerra and soon to be leader of the Martelé?"

"Because I am not any of those things." Leo relaxes and lies down on the blanket beside me. He taps the area at his side for me to lie down too. "Marco will continue to lead the Guerra. And Alex and Vanna will lead the Martelé as the *Martelé*."

I'm confused. "So, Alex is going to *be* a Martelé?"

Leo frowns. "It seems that way."

"But the Martelé are cruel. The way they treat women and children—it's immoral, disgusting."

"Vanna said she will change that. She wants to remodel the whole organisation. How easily and quickly she will be able to do that is her problem."

"Wow." I lie completely flat on the blanket and look at the sky, taking it all in.

Leo climbs on top of me and places his forearms on either side of my head. "Most importantly, it means that since there is no longer a feud between the Martelé and Guerra, there is no bounty on our heads." Leo kisses my forehead.

But I'm not convinced. I rise up, gently removing him from my body and pushing him back on his side. "Do you really think the Martelé who have hated the Guerra for years are just going to forget about it all?"

"No. There will always be chance of a rogue wanting to get one over on us. That comes with the blood, unfortunately. But there will be no payout for such an act, and that is what these assassins work for."

"What about him last night? Was he a Martelé?"

"No." Leo groans in displeasure. "He was one of ours. He hadn't been with the Guerra long. Van hired him because he was a ruthless killer. He has lived off-grid in Vietnam for ten years. There's no connection between him and the Martelé. Plus, if it was down to them, they would have made sure we knew about it so they could gloat. He just enjoyed inflicting pain and suffering on others for no other reason than to pleasure himself. He should never have been let anywhere near you and the boys. I'm partly to blame for that. I had no idea." Leo bows his head in shame.

I rub his back lightly, but I don't speak. We both just sit and watch Mark playing in the sand.

After noticing the time, I say, "Come on, let's get back. Dinner will be ready."

Leo looks at me with sympathy, and I remember that no, it won't. Leo wraps his arms around me as we stand. He holds me while I sob into his shoulder. This isn't fair. Alga and Serigo were the kindest, friendliest people I have ever met. They would do anything for anyone, and they did. They gave their lives for us.

When we return to the house, Van informs us that we have a visitor waiting at the gate.

"Who is it?" Leo asks.

"It's Sergio and Alga's daughter, Stephanie."

"Tell her we are busy and to come back another day." Leo dismisses.

"No!" I exclaim. "Leo, she has just lost her mother and father. You cannot send her away. She does know, right?"

"Yes, she knows. Marco informed her this morning," Leo explains.

"Does she know the truth?" I ask, worrying.

"I'm not entirely sure what Sergio and Alga told their daughter. I have never met her. I do know that she is a doctor and that she visited their home on the grounds quite often. Therefore, I assume she knows who they worked for."

"Oh yes, I remember. I did Alga's hair for her graduation. Then I think we owe her an explanation or whatever it is she has come for."

"I'll speak to her in my office. You take the boys upstairs." Leo says to me.

"No. Ask Van to watch the boys. We will both speak to her in the sitting room."

Chapter Fifteen

Leo

Katie has made tea and coffee and placed them on the coffee table. I can see she is trying to hold back her emotions while we wait for Stephanie to be shown into the house. I'm worried about my wife's heart with everything that has happened. Thankfully the medication the medics gave her last night have settled her blood pressure and heart, but the sooner I can get my family settled in a better environment, the better.

"Mr and Mrs Guerra." Van introduces us to Stephanie as he leads her into the room. "Stephanie, daughter of the late—"

Katie cuts him off. "Yes, Van, thank you. Please, Stephanie, come in. Take a seat, and please call us Katie and Leo."

"I will just stand if that's okay. I won't take much of your time." Stephanie looks just like her mother, though her hair is darker and her skin more olive, but the resemblance is certain.

Her eyes are glazed and her cheeks swollen with emotion.

"Stephanie," I begin. "Please accept my sincere apologies for the loss of your parents. They were both very highly regarded, and we thought of them more as family. Whatever you want to know or anything you need, please, it is yours."

"My only request is the cause of death on their death certificates. I don't know if you are aware, but I am high up in the medical field, and I know they would not want anything to jeopardise my future." Stephanies eyes fill with tears. She takes a deep breath and continues. "I'm sorry, I know it must sound very selfish of me to come here and ask for this, but my parents did everything for me. They worked so hard to give me everything I have got, and they would be heartbroken if anything they had done ruined that."

"We understand," Katie sympathises.

"I know who you are and what you do. And while I have never felt comfortable with my parents working for you, I know how highly they thought of you and how well you treated them. If it wasn't for your loyalty and kindness to them, I would not be where I am today."

This is not how I thought this conversation was going to go.

"I therefore know it will be within your

power to arrange the death certificates as I wish."

"It is something I can arrange. Have you a reason in mind?"

"Yes. My mother had terminal cancer. Twelve months ago, she was given six months to live. Obviously she surpassed that. At six months, she was still going, and she refused to stop working, as she said that was what was keeping her alive. She said her time wasn't up until she was ready."

"Oh, Stephanie, I'm so sorry. We had no idea."

"That was how she wanted it. She wanted to be treated the same, not as a dying woman."

"She was an amazing woman," Katie agrees.

"The diagnosis broke my father's heart. I know that he did not want to live without her." Stephanie sobs and wipes her face with her hands.

Katie passes her a tissue and stands beside her. "I'm so sorry, Stephanie."

"I guess what I am trying to say is, I don't want to know any details. My mother died of her terminal illness, and my father died of a broken heart. They are both at peace together, and all I ask is that the paperwork reflects that."

"Done," I agree.

"Thank you." Stephanie breathes a sigh of

relief.

"Your mother and father had a pension and life insurance with us. That will of course go to you. They lived in the house on our grounds, which will need to be emptied. We can leave that until you are ready."

"Here, this is my number, and this is Leo's. Let us know if there's anything else you need."

"Okay. I'll be going now."

Katie shows her out, and I retreat to my office, pour myself a scotch, and light a cigar. The guilt I felt for the death of Alga and Sergio has lessened slightly now that I know that Alga was terminally ill. But Sergio still had years ahead of him. Then again would he have wanted those years without his wife? It's a decision I hope I never have to make.

I turn on my computer, login into the Guerra accounts, and wire a one-million-pound transfer to Alga and Sergio's account. This will then get passed on to Stephanie. Better to not send it straight to her, as she won't want any connection to us.

Katie appears at my door looking panicked. "Marco is coming down the driveway with my parents."

"Come here." I wave her over and stand from my desk. "It's going to be emotional and hard. It may take time, but they will get there. We all will."

Katie takes a deep breath and nods.

"And luckily, we have two amazing boys that will steel their hearts in an instant," I add.

"Yes—oh my goodness, they are grandparents, and they don't even know it."

"We'll keep them upstairs until you're ready. Remember, you tell them as much as you think they can handle. I'll be by your side as always." I hold her face and kiss her firmly. She starts to melt in my arms like she always does, but I pull away, turn her round, and smack her ass before her parents see their next grandchild being conceived.

We wait in the sitting room for Marco to bring them in. Katie cannot settle and is pacing the room, biting her nails. She stops when she hears the front door open.

We can hear Katie's father protesting, accusing Marco of kidnapping and some sort of sick joke. He still obviously doesn't believe it. As a father, I can imagine the pain he must be going through.

Marco enters the room first, with Katie's parents, Paul and Heather, close behind him. Marco's large frame covers their view until he steps aside.

Paul's eyes land on me first. They widen in disbelief, and then they then land on Katie, who stands at my side. His expression is one that I am sure will stay with me for the rest of my life. The colour drains from his face. The idiom *he looks like he has seen a ghost* is a correct way to describe it. He is frozen because the daughter he mourned has in fact returned from the dead.

"Oh, Katie," Heather gasps. "How, why?" She screams with emotion and runs towards Katie. She puts her hands on her daughter's face, kissing her cheeks as if to check she is real.

Paul continues to stand and watch, not saying a word. I wonder whether to say something to him. But I'm not sure what I would say.

"Is it really you?" Heather continues.

"Yes, it's me, Mum."

There's a sound from Katie's father that I can only describe as a wail. He bends and puts his hands on his knees.

Worried he may pass out, I go to him.

"Come and sit down." Gently, I put my arm under his and lead him to the sofa.

Katie sits down beside him, her mum clinging on to her arm as if she may disappear again. "Dad. Are you okay?"

"I didn't believe it. I can't believe it. We had your funeral." He cries and puts his head in his hands.

"I'm sorry, Dad. We had no other option."

"But why? Why did you do this? Oh, I can't believe this." He's short of breath, and I think he may be having a panic attack.

"Marco, bring us some water and refreshments," I command.

After comforting him for a moment, Katie says, "Here, drink this." She hands her dad a glass of water from the tray Marco has just plonked down on the table. He doesn't like being a server. "I want you both to just listen while I explain. Then you can shout and scream at me or ask any questions, but let me just get it all out first."

Katie begins by explaining why the Martelé wanted us dead. That it was them who kidnapped her back in London and that I had killed their leader, so this was their revenge. She explains how I had planned it all to keep her safe and that she had no knowledge of it until it happened.

"I was heartbroken. I lost everyone I loved. I wanted to tell you, but I had to keep you safe. If you had known, you would have been in danger."

"There must have been another way. You could have gone to the police, couldn't you?"

"Dad, please let me finish," Katie pleads. "There was no other option. But now that things have changed, we have been able to return."

"But are you safe now?" Heather asks.

"Yes, we are safe now," I reply.

"You did this!" Katie's dad stands in anger. "You put my daughter's life in danger. Then you took her away!"

Marco steps forward, ready to restrain him. I put my hand out for him to stand down and give him the nod to bring down the boys. I think we need to diffuse the situation before it gets to be too much.

"Dad, please. Leo did all this to protect me. He saved me."

Katie's mother then starts to argue with her dad. "Can't you just be grateful to have your daughter back?"

"Mummy?"

Mark's voice interrupts the arguing. He runs to his mother, and Katie picks him up and gives him a cuddle. Katie's parents watch in shock.

"Mum, Dad. This is your grandson Mark."

Katie's mum starts to cry, and the angry red drains from Katie's dad's face.

"And this is Zander," I say, having taken him from Van's arms.

Heather immediately goes to Katie and Mark. Tears stream from her eyes.

"Hello, Mark." Heather sniffs through tears.

Marks shyly hides his face in Katie's

shoulder, probably a little taken aback by Heather's emotion. Katie wraps her free arm around her mother.

"Mark, this is your grandma. She's not sad. She's just very happy to meet you."

Mark lifts his head slowly to look at her.

"It's okay, Mark. It's a lot to take in for me too." Heather smiles at my eldest son.

"Would you like to hold Zander?" I say to let Mark have a minute to adjust.

"I'd love to." Heather takes Zander from my arms, and her face lights up. "He's got your nose, Katie," she says as she kisses to top of his head. "Look, Paul. Look how much he looks like Katie when she was a baby." Heather turns to Paul, who is still staring at the situation in front of him. His mouth opens slightly, like he's not quite believing what he is seeing.

"Come on, Grandad. Come and meet you grandsons," Heather pushes him.

For a minute, I think he is going to refuse, but then he laughs.

"Grandad. Me, a grandad." His face breaks into a big smile, and he stands and joins us.

Zander is then passed between each grandparent, both of them wanting to hold him as much as possible. They both slowly gain Mark's trust and have him showing them his latest favourite toy, a train that Alga and Serigo got for him when we arrived.

After a few hours of catching up, Mark is playing in the garden with his new grandad, and Zander is being given copious amounts of cuddles.

I can see my wife is getting tired, so I interrupt. "We know this has been a lot to take in. It will take a long time for us all to adjust. But we would both be very happy if you would be part of our future, especially the boys. I have booked you in at a nearby hotel, and we would like it if you would join us again tomorrow."

Katie smiles at me, appreciating my words. Paul and Heather are grateful for my invitation and excitedly promise to return tomorrow. I'm relieved that Katie's parents finally know the truth, and I'm happy it went as well as can be expected for Katie. Hopefully she can start to relax more now.

Katie

Once my parents leave to go to their hotel, I breathe a sigh of relief. I'm completely drained. After an emotional and difficult start, we had a really lovely afternoon. Dad played football and catch with Mark for hours, and Mum sat and cuddled Zander so much, I'm worried he won't want to be put down now. Before that, we sat outside, and they filled me in on their lives from the past few years.

It was painful listening to their sorrow of losing their daughter and the struggles they've been through. But hopefully now we can spend a lot of time together and start creating new memories.

One very surprising and good thing (I hope) to come out of all of this is that my parents are in a relationship. It was strange seeing them so comfortable in each other's company. Ever since I can remember, my parents have always been apart. They were very young when they had me. My dad was always the more sensible one, while my mum had her fair share of boyfriends when I was growing up. Most of them she was just with for their money. Whenever Mum and Dad got in the same room together, they would always bicker like they were teenagers again. But something has changed. They have matured. Their shared grief brought them back together. They were even talking of moving here to Italy. It's early days, but I am feeling very hopeful about our future as a family. I've really missed them. I've missed being part of a larger family, having people to talk to and experience things with.

When I go down into the kitchen the next

morning, I'm met with a familiar smell of freshly baked goods. I'm shocked to see a tall woman preparing food in the kitchen.

"Ahh, good morning, dear." The lady is English and has a very big smile and warm aura. "You must be Mrs Guerra. I'm Poppy. It's so lovely to meet you." She wipes her hands on her apron and offers one to me.

"It's lovely to meet you too. Please call me Katie."

"As you wish."

"I'm Mark." Mark holds his hand out to Poppy.

"Well, how do you do, Mark?"

Leo appears behind us.

"Good morning, Mr Guerra."

"Good morning, Poppy. I see you have met my family. This is Poppy. She is the new housekeeper."

"Housekeeper, cook, washerwoman, you name it. I'll make sure I look after you all."

"Thank you. We are pleased to have you here," I lie, missing Alga and Sergio. I'm sure Poppy is very lovely, but the place just doesn't feel the same without them.

"Right, everyone. Have your breakfast and get dressed. I have a surprise for you." Leo grabs

one of the freshly made croissants off the island,
takes a bite, and leaves the room.

Chapter Sixteen

Leo

"Where are we going, Papa?" Mark asks as he strains to look out of the car window.

"It's a surprise."

"What's this all about?" Katie puts her hand on my leg as I drive.

"You'll see when we get there." I'm sure they are going to love it. At least I hope they are. I make a sharp left turn in Marco's brand-new four-seat Ferrari. He wasn't happy about loaning me his new toy, but I gave him no option. I may purchase one of these myself. Its powerful, throaty rumble is addictive.

We pass Van going in the opposite direction, obviously having finished my requests just in time. When we reach the end of the tree-lined road, we come up to a wooden gate. One thing that still needs to be replaced. I get out and open it, hoping the new electric security one will be fitted tomorrow.

When I get back in the car, Katie is frowning and pouting. I love when she makes this face. I laugh because I think she has an idea of why we are here, having noticed the post box to the side of the entrance. Once we are through the gate, the house is in sight. It's a large double-fronted cottage that has recently been renovated by the previous owners. They weren't planning on moving, but I had other ideas. The car jerks to a stop—I'll have to get used to the sensitive brakes.

Katie and Mark stare out of the window.

"Who lives here, Papa?"

"Come on, let me show you."

Once we are all out of the car, I carry Zander while Katie holds Mark's hand and heads to the front door.

"No. This way." Pointing to the side gate, I lead them around to the back of the house.

The sun is blinding when we walk into the large open garden that stretches down to a white sandy beach.

"I can see the sea!" Mark jumps up and down.

"It's beautiful." Katie shields her eyes to take it all in.

"And if you look to your left..."

"Is that a vineyard?"

"It certainly is. Come this way." I take Katie's

hand and lead her and Mark around to the right. Even Zander is wide awake taking it all in.

"It's Upsy and Daisy!" Mark jumps for joy at the sight of this billy goats.

"And chickens!" Katie cries. "Is this ours?"

"If you want it to be. Here we can have our family time again. But this time we have all our other family and friends close by."

"It's perfect, Leo. Thank you."

"Come on inside." I open the back door of the house and lead Katie and Mark inside.

"It's just like our house, Papa."

"That's because it is our house," I reply enjoying the happiness on my son's and wife's faces as they look around. The rooms are bigger than in our previous home on the island, but the layout is very similar. I've had the walls and soft furnishings changed to the same as we had, so Katie and Mark will feel right at home.

"This is my room." Mark explores his bedroom while I show Katie the rest of the upstairs.

"Both boys' rooms join on to ours, and each have their own bathrooms. I managed to replace most of the toys Mark had, and I've made a good start on things for Zander, but I'll need your help with the rest."

"I think you have done an amazing job. Thank you, Leo. This is wonderful."

"And I'm not sure how serious your parents were about moving here, but I've bought the next house as well, half a mile away, which is theirs if they want it."

Katie wraps her arms around me tightly, Mark then joins us, so I pick him up to join the embrace. I stand with my arms wrapped around my wife and two sons, my whole world.

Katie

The house is perfect. My spirit feels lighter now we are here. It's like my muscles have been tensed the whole time we have been back in Italy, and now they have finally relaxed. "Can we move in right away? Like, today?" The thought of spending another night in that house where Alga and Serigo died makes me tense up again.

"Of course. The place is ours. We do, however, have to go back the Guerra house tonight for an event."

"An event?"

"Yes. Marco and Mia—well, Mia really—are throwing a welcome home celebration for us and Alex and Vanna. She's going all out—friends, family, connections. You name them, they will be there. It's more of a declaration of power really. We need to be there, unfortunately. But we will go just to show our faces and then return here, to our home."

"Okay. And then that's it for a while? Back to family time?"

"Promesso." *I promise*.

"I need to find something to wear, then," I say, knowing full well that wardrobe in my new bedroom will be full of beautiful dresses. "What should the boys wear?"

Leo has a beaming smile on his face as reaches into the boys' wardrobe and pulls out the two matching three-piece suits and ties, one in Zander's size and one in Mark's.

"I knew they would need these for something." Leo winks.

The evening is actually very enjoyable. It's a true Guerra event with no expense spared. Everyone is dressed up, the drinks are flowing, food keeps appearing out of nowhere all fancy on silver trays, and the music has everyone dancing.

My parents come along, and it's so lovely being with them and Leo's family and friends. My mother and Leo's mother are actually getting along, and my dad seems to have calmed now. We have a lot of special people around us, and I never thought I'd say this, but I'm actually glad to be back. The boys' lives will be so much better, surrounded by all these people who love them.

Hopefully this will continue our happily ever after.

Thank you so much for reading

If you have enjoyed my books please connect with me on social media. I love to hear readers thoughts on characters and storylines.

There's lots more to come in this series so keep in touch.

You can also sign up to my email list which will keep you updated with my latest releases and offers.
Find me at www.joymullettauthor.com

Acknowledgement

To my wonderful parents.

Thank you for your love and encouragement and for helping me believe I can achieve anything in the world.

I am so grateful you are mine.

About The Author

Joy Mullett

Joy Mullett has turned her obsession with reading into writing. Being a lover of romance with a big imagination, Joy writes exciting and thrilling stories which are impossible to put down.

Follow Joy on Tiktok, Instagram and facebook.

Printed in Dunstable, United Kingdom